SERIO-COMIC
VIGNETTES

Kamran Ahmad

KINDLE DIRECT PUBLISHING

Serio-Comic Vignettes

Copyright © 2020 by Kamran Ahmad

All rights reserved. No part of this book may be reproduced by any mechanical, photographic, or electronic process, or in the form of phonographic recording; nor may it be stored in a retrieval system, transmitted, or otherwise be copied for public or private use-other than for "fair use" as brief quotations embodied in articles and reviews, without prior written permission of the publisher.

Dedication

In loving memory of my parents,
My wife Zunerah
and children Mahad and Saliha

About the Author

He hails from Pakistan and has served in the Civil Service of the country for more than 26 years. His main areas of interest include management and communication skills. He has an abiding interest in literature, humour and satire and believes in exploring new and exciting frontiers of life. He loves the energetic pleasure of sports and revels in the joys of fitness and exercise. Jogging, swimming, listening to music, solving cross word puzzles, playing cards and scrabble, reading, teaching, travelling and watching good movies are among his favourite pastimes.

Contents

Introduction 1

Lazy Eyes 4

Pillar of Pride 6

A Revelation 7

Somewhat Bruised 9

Not Insured 11

Visiting Card 13

A Hen-Party 15

Capital Punishment 16

No Difference 17

Leg Pieces And… 18

It Takes A Tie To… 19

Checking the Parts 20

A Mask 22

A Difficult Question 24

Women Are…	26
Know thyself	27
Head for Breakfast	28
Sick of Home	30
Telling Lies…	31
Trade of Tricks	32
The Other Four	33
Promoting Tourism	34
A General's Angle	35
The Evil Around Us	36
An Instructor's Take-On	38
Sense of Gratitude	39
Brevity Is The…	40
Labour Day	41
An Honest Custodian	43
A Stubborn Singer	45
An Apple A Day	46
A Horror Movie	47
Czech Women	49
Jump from A Much…	51
In Search of a Better Device	54
Flowers Can Hurt	55

Last Warning	57
Nothing Gained	59
Breaking the Law	60
Married Alive	62
Virtues of A Black Belt	64
All Trouble and No…	66
Dancing Away the Blues	67
Good for Nothing	70
Still Happy	71
First Date	72
Inch Vs A Mile	74
Price for Promotion	75
Two-Timing	77
An Interesting Law	79
Hiding from Oneself	80
Politics of Desire	82
Belle Époque Years	84
Saving Utensils	86
Settling Scores	88
Defying Explanation	89
A Marital Slice	91
College Days	93

Gains from An Accident	95
Wonderful Absence	96
Seven-Year Itch	98
A Bathroom Singer	100
Spotlight On…	102
Rebels Without A Cause	105
Honeymoon Days	108
Mirror Work	109
Hair Loss	110
Look Before You Leap	112
Watching A Movie	114
Remembering Good Things	116
Short-Sightedness	117
An Exercise in Futility	119
Some Tidbits	121
Second Cup of Tea	124
Lust at First Sight…	126
Unnecessary Demand	129
Clinging to Youth	130
An Emotional Punching Bag	131
A Movable Asset	133
Think Tank	134

What Are Wives For…	135
Match-Making	136
Escaping From…	138
Mother's Day	139
One Down and Nine to Go!	140
Being Oneself	142
Ransom for Handsome	144
You Too…	145
The Unfaithful H…	147
A Minor Operation	150
Robbed Of…	151
Homework Blues	152
Appearances Could Be…	153
My Name Is Not…	155
Prices and Wives Are	156
A Courteous Nation	158
The Moon Needs A…	159
Kingdom of Darkness	160
A Monk in the Making	163
Food for Thought	166
Television Vs A Hubby	168
Pronunciation Issues	170

Conscience – Go Fly A Kite 171

Dream-Man 172

Family Circus 174

French Are Great! 175

Female Psychology 176

A Hopeless Bald 178

Fleeting Glimpses 180

Issue of A Closet 182

Whose Fool? 183

Petrol Crisis… 184

Candid Talk 186

A New Lease on Life 188

Acknowledgements 190

References 191

Introduction

"Serio-Comic Vignettes" is predominantly a collection of comical-satirical pieces based in many cases on real life occurrences with a fair measure of my own touches. A lot of stories are also based on my own experiences and observations. Some of the incidents chronicled in this work were shared with me and stem from what was essentially encountered or recounted by others. I have tried to make use of my imaginative faculties in suitably developing the narrative details of those situational settings and occurrences. Wisecracking, sarcasm, wordplay and pun are just a few genres of humour that lend piquancy to human experience.

The work constitutes an ample diversity of funny/interesting situations spanning over a long period of time. The items have for their setting – student life, marital tidbits, work place, social get together and a host of other amusing and spicy slices of life and chronicle a wide array of circumstantial and experiential reality. In many stories, the protagonist could be seen as struggling both externally and internally with the locus of control, amidst varying situational factors and ongoing personal conflicts. In a lighter vein, they showcase human nature with its vanities, foibles, eccentricities-idiosyncrasies, knack for the ridiculous and yearning to be understood and appreciated.

Elements of absurdity, witticism and drama are deeply woven into human psyche and situation. In real life, tragedy and comedy forever swap roles and at times the bitter-sweet cocktail of life becomes a wee bit hard to swallow. Much of human condition is marked by a comic appeal coupled with a firm touch of sobering reality. It does us good every now and then to drop our guard and give laughter a welcoming space in our recreation-starved lives. Laughter symbolizes joie de vivre, reinforcing feelings of well-being and is believed to have therapeutic properties. A feverish and unrelenting pace of activity in the post-modern times and a concomitant increase in stress and strain has wrought havoc on people's physical and psychological health. It has become all the more advisable to take things easy and lighten up a bit and also to salvage one's identity from the debris of daily clutter. It is worth one's while to occasionally escape from the monotony of over-structured days. Stealing time for oneself is one's birthright and should be jealously guarded.

People dowered with a sense of humour and the ability to look at the funny side to things are generally better equipped to take on frustrations, setbacks and failures with aplomb and equanimity. Put another way, their attitude enables them to take a brighter and cheerier view of things in the midst of trying circumstances and this way they are able to roll with the punches, keep their sanity intact and find a foothold to survive and eventually prosper and succeed.

The work is brimming with a multitude of voices – inner, judgemental, rebellious, naughty, satirical, farcical, comical, philosophical and serious, confident and shaky, sad and happy. They mirror the multifarious facets of human nature and situation.

Lazy Eyes

In a room filled with flowers, music, friends and laughter, orchestrated to commemorate the first wedding anniversary of a friend of mine who was a known chronic bachelor, I was immersed in a pool of thoughts – mulling over my past mistakes, reflecting upon the elusiveness of human contentment, twists and turns of an inscrutable fate and roles less travelled. *One is usually helpless before Destiny's cast of the dice and at times the hunter becomes the hunted; I divined while being gently rocked by the ebb and flow of a meditative mood. Were my hard-to-explain inhibitions keeping me from reaching out to others?*

In a far corner of the room a musician was passionately playing the trombone to pep up the event. On the wall behind him was a painting of a swan and cygnets swimming in tow on the aqua-blue waters of a pristine lake.

After complimenting the couple and presenting them with a bouquet of red roses, I gave free reins to my pent-up curiosity and sizing up my friend said, "Your sudden metamorphosis in a year plus time from a celibate to the one savouring the fruits of marital bliss is truly remarkable". "Everything", I continued in the same breath, "seems to have dramatically changed in the blink of an eye".

"My dear", he quipped, "your eyes take too much time to blink!"

Pillar of Pride

Chatting during a break in the office tea-bar, someone suggested that let each of us say a word or so about our weaknesses. The idea was excitedly bought and everybody was quite forthcoming. It helped in appreciating each other on a more realistic and humane plane and lightened the burden of carrying false appearances in a world riddled with hypocrisy and duplicity. *Much of our social persona is masked by a charming facade of friendliness.*

Wanted a fairy to appear, pull out a wand and offer me three wishes. First wish: Craved for a holiday in the sun with an old flame of mine…

When my turn came, in a bid to appear humorous, I quoted a famous one-liner, "Of all the things I have lost, I miss my mind the most".

The pillar of my pride came crashing down when a colleague with a cynical gleam in his eyes promptly added, "But I wonder, how you could possibly lose anything you never had in the first place!"

A Revelation

Having totally forgotten about a piece of work assigned to me by my wife while leaving for office in the morning, I was stumped for a plausible excuse as I rang the doorbell of my house in the afternoon. A pale-orange sunlight was cresting across the horizon. Up in the yonder a plane droned on through a tranquil sky. Adjacent to the doorbell, I saw gold-yellow and mauve-coloured butterflies fluttering around the bougainvillea adorning the entrance door. I was belting out a song to keep my spirits up – trying to maintain a carefree charade. *I wonder much like others: Are we all following our pre-determined destinies? Wish I could go shopping 'reasons' for so much that remains unexplained. Floundering in personal uncertainties I was gripped by the impulse to drop everything and build a new life...* After a while, the door opened and my wife with a towel turbaned around her head greeted me and smilingly inquired about the chore. Licking and biting my lips and scratching my head, I somehow confidently manufactured what appeared to me quite a convincing explanation.

Pointing a finger towards me and without mincing words she gave her verdict, "You are telling a lie!" Her eyes appeared like tips of a sword.

Slightly taken aback by her blunt accusation, I nevertheless kept my cool and in a light-humoured tone asked, "How did you judge that I was lying?"

Her answer came as a complete surprise to me was, "It's very simple, whenever you tell a lie you become more good-looking".

Somewhat Bruised

A few years back my wife and I attended the wedding ceremony of one of my cousins, which was held in one of the posh hotels of Islamabad. After reaching the hotel, we found ourselves in the midst of a jam-packed hall where the function was in full swing. We started combing the crowd for suitable company. My better half spotted an elder female cousin of mine and struck up conversation with her. Basically, a boy and bachelor at heart and a libertarian by temperament, I decided to have my fill of fun by feasting my eyes (smouldering with desire) on the comely females thronging the place like mobile flowers. I was straining to make conversational gambits with some of them. I champion the view that in a social gathering, pretty females should sit in the lap of handsome men. I felt as a bad-boy genius all set to recruit damsels in the academy of forbidden pleasures. One of the girls had long hair, long arms, long legs… and I instantaneously developed a long…ing for her. *A cruise adventure with this girl would be helluva good fun!* Noticing my blatant self-indulgence my senior cousin in a lecturing tone advised,

"You are a married man and instead of playing a fox in the chicken coop, you ought to be a little more careful and discreet".

In a tone meant to tease my wife whose temper is generally on a short fuse and who happens to be quite possessive and aggressive, I airily said, "You see, I have rolling eyes and a roving heart". *Was my glad eye making my wife unglad? Maybe she needs to carry a circus whip in her hand to tame a tiger (read me) on the loose... A few points to ponder – some other day!*

Clad in a mischievous smile and reinforcing it by suggestively nudging my wife, whose eyes were already ablaze with fury, my cousin tilted her chin and looked into my eyes and in a quasi-serious tone said, "That we shall see tomorrow, when you will have a black eye and a bleeding heart!"

Not Insured

During a holiday trip to my native city Lahore – more than a decade ago, I was in a festive and freewheeling mood and threw all caution to the wind while gallivanting around the city with my wife on my brother's company-maintained car. *Live as you want – a thought that has always held me in thrall. Are we being selfish when we follow our own star? How many of our goals, interests, avenues of entertainment and satisfaction are sacrificed to gain (ever elusive) familial and societal approval??* Sensing my reckless driving my better half cautioned me, " Be careful, car accidents are a dime a dozen". She seemed like a cop from 'vice-and-virtue squad'. Overhead an orange-red sun appeared blurred by smoke and pollution.

Dismissing her concern with a careless wave of hand, I thoughtlessly remarked, " Nothing to worry, the car is company-maintained". Then slapping my thighs with gusto, I let loose an exuberant cheer and accelerated the speed of the car to feel young at heart. *Drop your worries, travel light…*

Giving me a half-amused and half-sober smile, she looked at me over the top of her glasses and evenly said, "Yes, I agree the car is company-maintained, but don't forget that we are not!"

Visiting Card

A research project assigned by the government, though predominantly a serious undertaking has its share of light moments. One day after a taxing mental drill at the office, we were having our fill of fun over a coffee break by exchanging jokes, raillery and puns – trying to reclaim our lives from the clutches of a cheerless routine. There is no time in life when a person does not need a little perking up. The repetitive rhythm of survival necessitate that we leap out of rut, loosen up and enjoy life. Light-hearted moments somewhat help in filling the vacuum of our inner lives and in overcoming to some degree the empty desperation of modern life – plagued by a sense of unfinished business and unlived life.

Fate appears to be an unkind bartender serving bitter drinks of black sorrow to many a customer most of the time… fairness doesn't seem to be its strongest suit. God moves in mysterious ways!

The image of a bear dancing to the beat of a drum raced through my mind.

Playing smart, one of my office colleagues having a macaw-like nose teasingly pasted a blank sticker note on my coat. Keeping the score even, I scribbled 'MR FOOL' on the same and glued it on his necktie for display.

Wearing a derisive smile, he topped it by bowing low in a mocking way and saying, "Thanks for your visiting card!"

A Hen-Party

At a hen-party with the usual setting – women engrossed in jabbering and backbiting, a young lady exhibiting glamorous confidence with honey-brown hair and caramel-coloured eyes presiding over a lithe physique – clad in a becoming dress smugly said, "My husband is completely under my control", then gulping down a tall mug of cold coffee hastily added, "and not only that he even sees the world through my eyes".

Upon hearing this, a middle-aged lady with an angel's face and a devil's grin, sitting nearby hunched forward and looked her in the eye and in an acerbic tone remarked, "I can bet my dear that he is going to become blind very soon!"

Capital Punishment

Two of my close friends have what may be called as a mock-insult relationship. They derive unholy pleasure from the keen swordplay of their wit and are always trying to get one-up on each other. Not long ago, both of them were seated in the T.V. lounge of my house and were engrossed in watching a programme, where the anchorman through show of hands, sought opinions for and against capital punishment from the audience. The opinion poll showed that the majority of audience was vehemently against capital punishment. Registering that, one of them invited the attention of the other and asked, "What is your opinion about capital punishment, shouldn't it be banned for good?" he strongly urged.

The snappy come-back of the other was, "Seeing you, I firmly hold that it should be there!"

No Difference

Two of my friends viz Sagheer and Kabeer, known for their wisecracking and scintillating wit were having tea at my residence and were hitting it off with each other. Suddenly Sagheer posed me with an unusual question, "What is the difference between Kabeer and a Chimpanzee?"

Playing it safe so as not to give offence to anybody and also taking heed of the predatory gleam in the eyes of Sagheer, I maintained a neutral stance and merely said, "I did not know".

Sagheer amid laughter sneered, "Of brain", further elaborating his point, he wagged his finger in Kabeer's face and remarked, "Chimpanzee has been blessed with a brain, while he lacks one".

Kabeer was not in the least put off by this stinging insult and maintaining an air of sophisticated weariness asked me, "Do you happen to know the difference between Sagheer and a chimpanzee?"

I was at a fault for an answer and feigned ignorance. His rejoinder was, "No difference!"

Leg Pieces And…

Once my friend and I were invited to a banquet hall, where the wedding dinner of our common friend was hosted to celebrate the occasion. The hall was festooned with flowers and lights – crowded with almost an equal number of males and (palpably-alive) females – who had let their hair down and unfurled a champagne-like liveliness that made the ceremony more enjoyable. The song 'hot stuff' by Donna Summer playing in the background added an extra zip to the function. *Most of the females were good from far and one could say not too far from good.* We were engrossed in small talk with some guests and after a while realized that the dinner had already begun. Let me point out that I have a special weakness for leg pieces of chicken and, therefore, impatiently aired my concern, "**Chop-chop!** Let's get on with the dinner, lest the leg pieces are finished". Leering at the females, he gave me a cheeky wink and remarked, "My dear, the leg pieces may be finished, but the breast pieces would still be available".

It Takes A Tie To...

During my post-graduate days in the Economics Department of Government College, Lahore, I am reminded of an interesting incident. Elections were held by way of voting to select a person for the Presidential slot of Post-Graduate Economics Society.

The two candidates aspiring for the post, namely Shahid and Kareem were almost equally popular and we knew that the competition would be neck and neck. I cast my vote in favour of Shahid, who had recently presented me with a necktie and was a kind of friend to me.

The announced results of the election unveiled an interesting scenario as Kareem had lost by just two votes. The exact position was that Kareem received 19 votes, while Shahid bagged 21. Taking stock of the situation, a class fellow of mine, who knew about the necktie affair clapped hands over his head and commented, "Shahid's tie, saved the tie!"

Checking the Parts

Engaged in a lively patter of talk, we drove one mellow evening towards my cousin's house, who after having spent the day with my wife was then keen to join her uxorious husband. It was nearly sunset and the tangerine sky looked hauntingly beautiful. The vibrant gold of evening sun stained the eastern sky with finely blended hues of pink, red, gold and orange issuing from the divine artist's palette. *For me there was a certain je ne sais quoi in the landscape. A caravan of images flitted across the screen of my mind... I drove on with my jumbled thoughts, staring listlessly into space – pondering over a life unfulfilled – wondering what the future had in store for me – confronting my smallness in Nature's scheme of things. Above in the sky, a lone kite fluttered its wings to stay afloat in a difficult world. I was yearning to go to some tiny picturesque village for complete rest to escape from the brutality of city life and over-structured days. There is no blinking the fact that it does us good, every once in a while, to break out of our compartments of worry and take a vacation from personal cares and responsibilities.*

Dear reader sharing with you (in camera) an eerie feeling = Sometimes I think I am going to wake up to find it was all a dream.

On reaching her place, I honked the horn and after a while her hubby, whose brow was lined with a perpetual frown, nervously appeared on the door, wearing a goofy look. We often ribbed him about his bald head and bulbous nose. He seemed tense as a violin string.

Poking his soft underbelly, I joked, "Look here Mister, we are returning your wife safe and sound, moreover in a single piece".

Chortling with amusement whilst winking at me, he clenched his shoulders up to earlobes and rejoined, "Well, that I can only tell after checking all the parts!"

A Mask

Sitting in the car, parked in front of a superstore, where my wife had gone to fetch some groceries, I was twiddling my thumbs and humming a tune to outwit boredom and while away the time. Fishing out the camera from the glove-compartment, I took my own half-face picture while winking at the camera. Looking above I could see layers of white billowy clouds floating along the horizon. For a while, I quietly observed cloud formations and felt awed by the infinite divine artistry. While casually surveying my surroundings, my eyes rested on a roadside monkey handler whose monkey was trying to please the onlookers by mimicking the appearance of a polished gentleman by stylishly putting on a hat, bow, sunglasses and a coat. *We are but socially acceptable versions of our core selves!*

In the backseat, my son was amusing himself by frightening his younger sister wearing Dracula's facemask.

Upon seeing her returning, I decided to have a little fun. I quickly impersonated Dracula by fixing its mask on my face and as she entered the car; I let out a menacing laugh and pounced on her, expecting to draw a cry of horror.

Proving herself one cool customer, she remained unruffled and sardonically remarked, "Do me a favour, keep wearing this mask!"

A Difficult Question

Being an average-looking man, at times I wistfully gaze into the mirror, while checking my appearance. On one such instance, I found my savvy wife standing right behind me, coolly studying me. *At times we wonder sadly about what might have been. Much of life is characterized by a nagging sense of incompleteness and why we have not been able to understand the meaning of life despite living? Yes, I was craving for a distraction from the listless boredom of existence and endless linearity of time. Ah! Our life is but a speck and our stay on earth but insignificant moments in the infinite design of cosmic mystery. This life – this patchwork of uncertainty, confusion, betrayals, regrets and disappointments... made me quietly sad. Have I been dealt a losing hand – much like so many others? The mirror seemed to reflect my inner torment.* Donning a jolly mood and confidently inflating the balloon of my vanity, I theatrically delivered my lines: "Oh God, why have you made me so handsome, utterly attractive and desirable?"

I let out a whoop of joy and thrust my right hand up!

Without batting an eyelid and maintaining a Zen-like calm, she dropped a brick, "Honey, why do you ask God such difficult questions!!"

Women Are…

Hen parties where ladies generally let it all hang out are among my wife's favourite pastimes. "What took you so long?" was the question I fired at her point-blank, when she came back home quite deep into the night from one such get together. Slipping into a thoughtful mood as if trying to replay the evening in her mind's eye, she looked a bit like an Oxford professor pondering a tricky point as she gave her answer, "I had every intention of leaving the party early", "but my dear one", she continued, "they spoke so ill about all the women who left that I had no heart to say goodbye till all of them had gone".

Know thyself

On a visit to an Army Aviation Squadron, a friend of mine hiding behind a pair of dark glasses accompanied me. It was a bright day under a cobalt sky. We were surprised to see that the Aviation Squadron was literally studded with signposts carrying flight safety slogans and guidelines. One particular signpost caught the attention of my friend. It read, "Knowledge is the most powerful tool of flight safety, know your aircraft like you know yourself". Resting his left cheek on the palm of his left hand, he reflected upon it and commented, "I do not agree with it, as one does not know oneself at all". "Remember", he added blowing out his cheek, "Know thyself – the most difficult lesson".

Head for Breakfast

It was a fine Sunday morning characterized by low tones and a delicious laziness and one could see puffy white clouds lingering on a porcelain blue. My wife and I were both feeling lethargic, as it was a weekly holiday and we both had overslept. We were sitting in the garden of our home and had just woken up and were busy gathering our senses about us, knuckling our eyes and trying to break through the cobwebs of sleep. A helicopter was whining overhead. I tried to enliven my mood by lighting a badly needed cigarette....I was lolling in the shade, gazing indolently at the unkempt garden – inclined to laze away the day. I'm all for a languid rhythm of life… think of me as a combat-weary sailor in search of calmer waters. How tempting it is to lead a frivolous, thoughtless life – without having to make sense of your fate in a throwaway world. I was sitting, leaning a bit forward, with my left-arm elbow resting on my left leg and my left palm covering half of my face and eyes were fully closed… Shut out the world that mars our peace and happiness and dumps us in our darkest hours. *Unspoken words hung in the air like still puppets – yet to be shocked into life by a weary puppeteer who seemed to have given up the hope of ever producing the desired results.*

Interestingly, none of us was in the mood to prepare the already belated breakfast. For good form's sake and in a non-committal tone, I asked my wife, "What would you like to have for breakfast?"

Pulling a morose face, she darted a contemptuous look at me and caustically said "Your head!"

Sick of Home

It was a memorable experience to undergo a one-month group-training course at Tokyo International Centre, Japan in the year 2000. Participants from across the globe were gathered there. Despite the fact that in a new environment, there is so much to see, learn and sample, it was beyond my grasp as to why most of the participants were homesick and consequently went through their days with almost a sense of tiresome obligation. To beat the blues, one evening we were sitting in a bar – filled with the gusto of life and enjoying beer with cocktail music when one such participant wearing a wide-brimmed brown hat and having a banana-shaped nose asked me, "Aren't you feeling homesick?"

"Me", "Not at all" was my crisp response.

His cracker of a reply was, "Then, you must be sick of home!"

Telling Lies...

The other day sitting under a whirring ceiling fan, I was trying my prentice hand at singing one of the favourite songs of my wife and since I am a pathetic singer was making a poor fist of it, much to my wife's chagrin. Making an audible groan, she pleaded with me to stop, but enjoying her annoyance, I continued butchering the song. To carry the fun forward, I asked her to praise my good voice and singing skills and insisted that in order to please me, she might tell a lie (every) now and then. Bursting into peals of laughter, she shot her quip; "In that case, I would be telling lies all the time."

Trade of Tricks

It was a jewel-like day with a turquoise sky adorned with cottony clouds as I ran into a friend of mine, who after having completed his education was undergoing apprenticeship at his father's business firm. Seeing him, I casually remarked, "So these days, you are learning the tricks of the trade"

Flashing me a sly smile whilst scratching his left cheek with his (right) index finger nail, he chimed in, "On the contrary, I am learning the trade of tricks".

The Other Four

In our country, it is not unusual to come across names that are quite long. One day in our Mathematics class, during my student life, the teacher was taking roll call and called aloud a name (Syed Nauman Ali Haider Gardezi). From the back of classroom, a voice piped up, "I am here sir".

The class broke into a hearty laugh, when the teacher promptly inquired, "Where are the other four?"

Promoting Tourism

During our pre-service training program conducted in Civil Services Academy, two days were earmarked for syndicate report presentations by the trainees' on assigned research topics. These presentations were to take place before a sizeable audience and all trainees were required to attend the proceedings.

Our turn was on the second day and topic was, "Development of tourism in Pakistan". On day one, our syndicate in charge, a female instructor, noticed that majority of our syndicate members were missing and in an annoyed tone asked me the reason of their non-availability. Half-confident, half-worried and gathering my wits, I pointed out, "Madam, the absence of our syndicate members shows their interest in tourism".

All was forgiven!

A General's Angle

A Pakistani general, reputed to be averse towards young army officers with bulging bellies, was once inspecting a final rehearsal prior to the grand armed forces parade that is held annually, on the occasion of Pakistan's Republic Day (23rd March) with great fanfare and pomp.

The general's surveying eyes spotted a young officer with a noticeably protruding belly. Looking him up and down and pointing a swagger-cane towards him in a taunting way, the general mocked, "Hey, are you a regular soldier or a makeshift?" Puffing up with pride, the officer replied, "Sir, I am a born gunner".

Somewhat amused, the general scornfully said, "Well, my dear gunner, I very much pity the gun, the poor gun, that gave you birth".

This led to a subdued giggling fit among the soldiers.

Sensing it, the general hit his chin with the tightly clenched fist of his right hand and barked, "What are you laughing at, don't you have any sympathy for other's pain!"

The Evil Around Us

One of my friend's (Raja) face is a testament to Nature's cruel joke and he looks quite horrifying during night-time. His ashen face, darkly ominous eyes, scarred cheeks, weird hairdo, ghastly looks and an emaciated physique made him a fit candidate to get a 'License to haunt'. We call him – *horror at large*. He is often made the butt for coarse jests on that account. During a recent get together of common friends (held around 8 p.m in the lawn of my house) including Raja, we were discussing supernatural phenomena like ghosts, evil spirits, apparitions et al and their impact on human life. A platinum moon hung in the sky – spangled with stars. Keeping us company was a group of noisy crickets – voicing their own fears. Then suddenly the insect orchestra ceased.

Making fun of Raja, a person squeezed his arm and remarked, "Whenever ghosts, evil spirits and their likes see you, I am sure, they are bound to get a big shock".

Not quite getting the point being made, Raja's face wore a demoniac expression as he stamped his foot and hissed, "What the devil does that mean?"

"It means", the guy added with a muffled giggle whilst giving him a quick jab with his elbow, "they feel at a loss to comprehend the fact that being undoubtedly one of them, you still manage to co-exist with human beings". "How come?"

An Instructor's Take-On

During a preliminary lecture on 'Economics', a young Instructor who happened to be single was explaining basic concepts such as needs and wants and ended up using these two terms interchangeably.

A somewhat confused student raised a query, "Sir, what is the difference between need and want?"

For a little while, the Instructor seemed baffled and his face went doll-blank, but then beaming an easy smile vivaciously said, "Well, it's quite simple to comprehend", and then brushing his lips with index finger continued, "You see, I want to marry 'Miss World', when all I need is a wife".

Sense of Gratitude

Aching to plumb the depth of my feelings, my wife one day posed a question, "Darling, what would you say to a man openly trying to seduce and then steal me from you?"

A curious smile began at the extreme corner of her lips.

Avoiding her piercing eyes and struggling to hold back my laughter, I muttered, *"Ummm… I should at least say Thank you!"*

Brevity Is The...

During a public speaking exercise at college, a student was assigned the topic 'Brevity is the soul of wit'. He ambled towards the rostrum, cleared his throat whilst smiling at the audience and simply uttered, "I agree with the topic" and strolled back to his seat amidst a chorus of applause.

Labour Day

On a flamingly fine day which happened to be May 1 (Labour Day) 2007, my censorious wife made me sit close to her as she peeled and chopped onions for cooking. *Aren't wives like onions too? But the catch is that when you peel them... all the layers appear monotonously alike.* Mired in a low mood, I was whistling to keep my spirits up and riffled through the pages of latest edition of 'Cosmopolitan Magazine' and used it to shield my watery eyes from further onslaught of onions' stench. It may be mentioned that my blurred vision made it quite difficult for me to properly appreciate the curves and contours of 'flavour-of-the-month' models teeming the pages of one of my favourite magazines. *Drifting off a little bit... I saw myself stranded on a tropical island with crystal waters and waving palms ... and I was running frantically... to escape the tyranny of huge-sized onions being hurled at me with an unusual force and accuracy by the same 'top models' populating the pages of ... Help!* **Help!** *I cried as one nasty onion after another chased me with the stubbornness of a sworn enemy...* Discombobulated by my day mare, I scurried back to the real world and wiped my overflowing eyes with a tissue. I angrily kept the magazine firmly shut as if trying to suppress the echoes of their high-pitched insulting laughter. Near the grate, our pet Alsatian was lying quietly as if brooding over the injustices of the world. *For how long would poor humanity continue matching steps to the soothing (yet cruelly deceptive) tunes of a jam tomorrow? And for quite a many living appears to be an insult… a punishment they didn't deserve and why fate is ever unwilling to lend a helping hand and take a lenient turn for many of us remains unexplained. How many times have I returned to the age-old, much debated, yet unresolved (fundamental) question: Is God above reasoning or is reasoning above God?? Life surely poses many questions, but provides few satisfactory answers. Isn't there a magic wand that can miraculously wipe away poverty and misfortune?*

Just then our telephone bell rang and my wife quickly picked it up and whispered that her mom was on the other line. Balancing the phone between her chin and shoulder, my wife took great delight in informing her mummy that her son-in-law for a change was in a tearful mood. Upon probably hearing the concern aired by my mother-in-law about my state of health and general welfare, my spouse smiled into the phone and in a jocular tone brushed aside her worry by saying, "All is well, I've made your spoilt son-in-law sit next to me while I'm engaged in chopping onions for lunch and believe me this is one surefire way of making an unfeeling person like him to cry once in a while!"

And I felt like running into a wall screaming, head first…!

An Honest Custodian

Within my social circle, I am known as a teetotaller and considered an honest custodian of alcoholic stock. A few years ago, a friend of mine, who is into drinking was having his entire house renovated and as a stopgap arrangement decided to deposit his sizeable alcoholic collection with me for safekeeping. I had the stock stacked safely in cupboards of my living room.

During that particular period, another friend of mine, fond of free and occasional drinking visited me and incidentally opened one such cupboard in my bedroom and found himself face to face with an impressive treasure of choicest liquor. Near the cupboard was a painting of a supine middle-aged woman in dishabille snoozing on the sand. Needless to say, he was instantly tempted to sample a bottle or two with a view to pick-himself-up and to get the better of a monotone mood that robs us of the excitement of life. *Any way you slice it, one big challenge in life is overcoming the 'not-feeling-up-to-it' inertia accompanied by finding clarity and coherence in the flux of living in a confusing world.* In fact, it was quite amusing to watch him virtually drooling over the spectacle as he raised himself on tiptoe with joy. But living up to my reputation, I put my foot down and stopped his inch by inch movement towards intoxicating beverages.

Taking a mental note of it, he frustratingly gesticulated at the invitingly open cupboard and bemoaned, ***"Whisky, beer everywhere, not a drop to drink!"***

A Stubborn Singer

Recounting the hilarity and camaraderie of college days when life was more of a merry-go-round… promising a pull out all the stops sort of excitement, I recall a class fellow of mine whose passion for singing was sadly hijacked by his unenviable voice and poor delivery which had more comic than entertainment value. Inexplicably, however, he never passed up a chance to sign in for performance whenever such an occasion arose. In a musical evening held at college, he prevailed upon the organizers to enlist his name among the singers. It would not be incorrect to say that he literally bulldozed his way to the event, partly to satisfy his monster-sized ego. And his ego was… one of God's most misplaced commodities.

Just before his turn in that show, he proudly informed a coterie of friends encircling him that he would be singing two songs – one 'happy' and the other 'sad'. Hearing this one of them in a burst of uncharacteristic bluntness said, "My dear this distinction is from your angle alone", then quickly surveying the audience added, "For the captive listeners both would be sad songs!"

An Apple A Day

During a post-prandial chitchat in the moon-drenched garden of our house, the other night, someone asked my sister-in-law as to why she was not having apples for afters. Her hubby, a doctor by profession, took over to reply with a tad of levity, saying: "Well, her reasoning is fair enough – an apple a day keeps the doctor away!"

A Horror Movie

Deeply absorbed in watching the horror movie titled 'I still know what you did last summer' one dusty evening, I was somewhat startled to hear the sharp ringing of phone bell. I was all by myself in the house as my wife and children had gone to spend the day at the residence of one of my wife's favourite cousins. *My imagination filled the silent house with people of long ago! My house had become as much a state of mind as a physical structure. Am I a reincarnation of my previous dead-self?*

Tottering on uncertain ground I gingerly walked towards the screaming gadgetry (that seemed to be venting its pent-up anger) and in slow motion picked it up. The low-pitched voice on the other line was of the hubby of my wife's cousin where my family was present at that time.

After exchanging the usual pleasantries, he casually asked, "What were you doing with yourself?"

I plainly told him that I was occupied in watching a horror thriller. I kept my eyes firmly shut. *Hounded by the arrows of a nightmarish reality, I took asylum in the comforting fortress of fantasy.*

"Why particularly a horror movie?" he inquired out of curiosity after a fairly long pause.

I let a trilling laugh break the spell of quiet enveloping the house before I disclosed my answer, *"**In order not to miss my wife's company too much and also to fill the vacuum created by her absence, I was consoling myself with a horror movie till her return!**"*

Czech Women

Introducing to me his wife – a Czech lady having deep-set eyes – ringed in kohl and thickly mascaraed , ruddy cheeks, cherry lips, a bright and breezy character and an hour-glass figure, with whom my cousin fell in love, while being posted in the diplomatic mission of Pakistan at Prague, my cousin remarked, "All Czech women are beautiful", and then with a faraway look in his eyes as if reminiscing about some bitter-sweet goodbyes, he breathed a sigh and in a deep bass voice added, "but I could take care of only one of them". She was wearing a gown of the colour of jacaranda blossom set off by an exquisite choker necklace and transmitted a regal grace and an unusual élan that instantly drew me towards her... she personified a living jewel! Her radiant trademark smile – straight from the heart – splashed across her glowing face. *Cupid had quickly shot an arrow straight through my h....*

She was the kind of woman one would love to be stranded with in a castle during a long hurricane.

I couldn't help but stare at the meltingly beautiful lady standing before me... she was fully capable of unleashing an emotional blizzard in a man and I felt enmeshed in the labyrinth of her seductively engaging charms... Was there a way out? I started daydreaming of cruising on a gondola along venetian canals... both of us in a tipsy, half-seduced state and sitting closely together, taking selfies... my left arm around her shoulder... her right arm resting on my left thigh... enjoying each other's company in a magical-romantic setting... losing track of time, the passing hours becoming a blur; one dreamy moment blurring into the next... the shimmering canal mirroring city's lights and our dreams... with the Venetian gondolier standing while paddling and steering and singing " O Sole Mio"... She seemed to have the uncanny ability of reading faces and minds and gave a smile out of the corner of her eyes to show she was not displeased.

It gave me a euphoric high. I tried to imprint the scene in my mind.

Giving him a hug, I whispered into his ear, "Congrats on becoming Czech-mated!"

Jump from A Much…

A pleasantly cool breeze caressed my face as I stood on the roof terrace (ten feet above the ground) of my residence enjoying the changing moods of nature and the luxury of free time, the other night. Lately the weather gods have been kind, I mused. I felt mesmerized by the celestial beauty of a scarlet moon adorning the dark sky. I philosophically stared into the pitch darkness – seeking to unravel night's best kept secrets – meditating over the enigma of life – questing for a greater sense of identity. *In a sophisticated world of false appearances, double-dealings and camouflaged intentions, I was a misfit and craved escape. I felt like a man in a canoe tumbling down the rapids, if it doesn't sink, it'll crash down the fall anyway. A sense of existential hopelessness engulfed me. At times, one feels worn out by the meaningless worldly trials hemming in one's life from all sides… a bit like a fictional being who has been pitch forked into a story where things are usually amiss and tragedies are lying just around the corner… Am I just acting out a script written for me before I was born? Are we mere playthings at the receiving end of fate's pranks?! Wish we were playwrights of our own lives – controlling its script, direction and outcome.* In the street overlooking the terrace, I saw an old beggar in rags muttering grievances and shaking his head. Then suddenly he became eerily quiet as if having lost his arguments before a sinister and unsparing fate. He vacuously stared into the distance – brooding about his paradise lost as he limped towards his usual destination knowing life was unlikely to deliver fulfillment and that he could do little except resigning himself to the bleakness of his existence. *How far a man could retreat into himself... hounded by a perennial grief? Oftentimes I've tried (albeit without much success) to decipher a conundrum: Are we all helpless spectators of our lives? How to escape the realities-cum-nightmares?? Both of us withdrew deeper into the wilderness of our respective resentments...* All of a sudden, an owl started hovering over the place – overcome with a bout of hooting – as if ridiculing the incompetent, insensitive, unjust and corrupt regimes of the contemporary world.

Just then my wife, well-known for her theatrics and often guilty of overplaying the emotional card crept up on me and derailed the train of my idle thoughts by shouting **Boo!** Upon noticing that I was rather unfazed by her gimmickry and simply unaffected by her presence, she threatened that she was going to jump from the terrace to end her uncared for life and to match her actions to the words comically proceeded to climb over the three and a half-foot high railing at the end of roof terrace – pretending to get away from it all.

"Please don't", I loudly said and pulled her back.

"How considerate of you", she said with a whoop of exhilaration and looked at me with thankful eyes.

"Och, Noooooo! You got hold of the wrong end of the stick, what I meant was that you ought to jump from a much higher place than this!" I said in a tone of mock exasperation.

In Search of a Better Device

Only yesterday I was telling a friend of mine by way of joke that the Japanese have produced a camera that has such a fast shutter speed that enables it to take a picture of a woman with her mouth shut.

Appearing unimpressed, he thumbed his nose at the idea and his mouth distorted in a lop-sided smile as he rasped, "It would have been far better if Japanese had come up with a device that could keep a woman's mouth shut – for good!"

Flowers Can Hurt

Engrossed in a creepy conversation with my cousin in his living room, while staying overnight at his place, some years ago, we were aghast at hearing a crashing sound that appeared to have come from one of the neighbouring rooms followed by a threatening howl let out by a stray cat. My eyes beheld a praying mantis seemingly glued onto the outer side of the window overlooking the garden and it appeared to be peeping inside as if spying on the inhabitants of the house. Shortly after, I saw my cousin's younger brother (Yawar – a 'go-against-the-grain' type) quickly entering the room… holding aloft a Jolly Roger flag and wearing an enigmatic smile matching well with an equally mysterious night. His limpid eyes mirrored a passionate celebration of life and he was always dreaming up some pranks to elevate the moment. His zaniness and an instinct to do something mindless set him apart from others. Out of rising curiosity, I inquired from him about the bang just heard by us. His face was still wreathing in smiles as he combed his hair with his right-hand fingers and in a muted tone replied, "Well, it has to do with my loving mom; she couldn't help hauling a flower at me out of overflowing affection".

"You must be joking". I stressed whilst shaking my head in a state of complete disbelief and then archly added, "I don't buy this explanation and obviously a flower cannot possibly make such a loud noise".

The penny dropped when he confided, "Actually that unkind flower was in a clay pot!"

Last Warning

Carrying a torch for someone may result in ... well, thereby hangs a tale.

During our Matriculation level, a lanky boy with plain face hidden behind thick specs tried to cotton (up) to a girl who could easily be described as pick of the class by wishing 'Good Morning' to her every day with a well-meaning smile.

She always kept her lips firmly sealed and grimaced at the boy who looked bewildered as a wingless crow. Her stock response was icy and her body language screamed – *stay away from me*. Yet the moth's infatuation for the flame continued unabated and he ill-advisedly kept on turning up like a bad penny and greeting her in the same manner daily.

Driven mad by these unwelcome overtures, the drop scene of this episode took place one day when the swain (wearing an embarrassed blush) continuing to latch on to her, routinely uttered, "Good Morning" whilst waving two fingers back and forth. Aiming a menacing finger at him and using her tongue like a rifle, she shouted, *"**LAST WARNING**!"*

Nothing Gained

"I have only gained more weight after my marriage"; my horizontally well-endowed youngest brother (now) weighing 130 kilograms informed a bunch of his close friends during a recent get together. A disarming forthrightness coupled with a self-effacing humour is among his trademark qualities. It was a sparkling day with a placid sky and overhead some birds flew past. We were sitting in a well-mowed lawn under the shade of a colourful umbrella and playing Scrabble. I saw a dog chasing butterflies. He was gazing pensively into the distance – as if trying to make some sense of the foibles and incongruities of daily life.

"Your Heaviness", someone inquired with a touch of sarcasm, "And what has your wife gained?"

"Nothing" he admitted freely as a wry smile conquered his big round face.

Breaking the Law

In our country, violation of traffic rules is more of a norm than an exception. Recently I happened to behold its classic example at a traffic signal crossing in Rawalpindi at an odd hour. I was flabbergasted to see two vehicles as if hell-bound breezing past the red light. It had a snowball effect and in the twinkling of an eye, a string of cars zipped past the red signal apparently without any compunction. Surely ethics have gone to the devil was the instant thought that crossed my mind. Looking sideways, I noticed a cat feverishly running as if trying to outpace some ravenous forces of evil and suddenly it disappeared into the serpentine arms of darkness.

Standing there all by my lonesome self, abiding the traffic norms, I felt every inch a fool in need of an overdue 'get-smart' counselling session. *Am I a discordant note in an otherwise smooth orchestra?* Then suddenly as if prodded by an evil impulse, I too turned a blind eye to the signal and quickly broke it to join the ranks of hard-to-tame Pakistani citizens, much to my wife's disapproval who violently shook her head as though to ward off an invisible swarm of mosquitoes. Shrugging aside the criticism, I justified my act by pointing out, "You see, when everybody is breaking the law, then nobody is breaking the law!"

Married Alive

My friend Tanveer is dowered with a photographic memory and has a gift for beautifully recounting a movie seen by him. Some years ago, at a birthday party of a common friend, he became the focus of attention as he masterly gave us a detailed rundown on a movie titled 'Buried Alive' recently watched by him. His blow-by-blow account of horror scenes showcasing darker side of human nature made us gasp with awe and kept our interest riveted. I found myself peering at a painting being reflected in the gilded glass over the fireplace showing a spooky cottage in a forest blurred by fog, smoke and a pervasive darkness. It cast an eerie spell on me... *through a film of grey mist I saw some ghosts pirouetting across the room... the walls of the house seemed to be closing in on me...* My heart did a double beat. Was my mind playing tricks on me?

Outdoors – thunder, lightning, rain and gust were playing games like petulant children.

One of our married friends who had been keenly listening to the creepy tale cut in, "I have been much inspired and can relate to the storyline and am thinking of making a movie that chronicles my own peculiar experiences".

"Wow! Sounds interesting!" Tanveer shouted like an excited child at a circus and then with a snap of fingers curiously asked, "What would be the name of the movie?"

A faint smile took over his deadpan face as he briefly mulled over it and then wearing an air of decent gloom earnestly said, "**Married Alive**!"

Virtues of A Black Belt

A distant relative of mine, whose two marriages had ended owing to physical abuse perpetrated by him on his hapless wives (one battered-half followed the other), visited me one day looking contrite. His eyes were pools of melancholy and his life seemed to have transitioned from a bed of roses to thorns. He was slouching on the sofa with his feet turned inwards and lips pursed. His posture betrayed weariness. I *guess the burden of negative emotional freight is not easy to carry.* He firmly assured that he had turned over a new leaf and sought my help in finding a suitable match – a girl who could redraw the emotional landscape of his life. Every relationship has its peaks and troughs and admittedly there are rough spots in almost every marriage, but his foray into this field up till now could only be described as a whirlwind of disasters. Like a tyrant, time rode roughshod over his dreams about happy blending of two lives and tragedy hung over his life like a stubborn autumn that simply refused to leave. He was desperate to snap out of his drab existence and earnestly promised to measure up to the criteria of 'MR RIGHT' and placed his right hand over his heart as a mark of pledge. *Did he deserve another bite of the cherry? I asked myself.*

He then became enclosed in a pocket of silence and contemplatively looked at a painting hung on one of the walls depicting a happy couple sauntering in a peaceful spot on the bank of a crystalline river. He gave a sigh and sank into a swamp of self-pity. Familiar with his poor marital scorecard, my wife who was clad in a live-hearted red dress and was toying with a heart-shaped blue-coloured balloon, gave him a wisp of a smile and wearing an air of ironic amusement said, "We hate to disappoint you, but we don't know any girl holding a black belt!"

All Trouble and No...

One of my friends is employed as a Course Commander in the National Police Academy that imparts pre-service training to newly recruited police officers. His job is an exacting one and mostly keeps him on his toes. Once I visited his office during duty hours and found him in the midst of giving operational guidelines to subordinates, taking directions from his superiors, attending to telephone calls, listening to and solving trainees' problems besides quickly leafing through office files requiring quick decision-making. Observing his stress-packed routine, I empathized, "Yours appears to be a trouble-shooting job."

Right behind his chair was the picture of a man dressed in Bermuda shorts; loose-fitting T-shirt, wearing a white Stetson hat and sandals relaxing in a chaise lounge on the edge of an emerald-coloured pellucid lake, holding a cold Heineken beer can in one hand and a Cuban cigar in the other.

Studying me for a while with his chin resting on his right-hand closed fist, he gave it a thought, "Let's put it this way, he said, "It is all trouble and no shooting!"

Dancing Away the Blues

To tide over a recent bout of despondency, I decided to dance for a while to music with a fast beat – trying to pluck out the thorn of worldly cares from my heart. *I wish there were 'Day Care Centers' for our troubles too!* Being a dancer with minimal skill and technique, I was clumsily hopping from left to right and vice versa and frantically wiggling my butt and swaying my arms to let off steam. My overall bodily movements were completely out of sync with the mood and rhythm of track being played.

Then a layer of fantasy took over… I found myself dancing in a discotheque teeming with merry makers, dreams, excitement, gaiety, colours… the heroine of my imagination ensconced in my arms… who wouldn't be sensuously inflamed by the wine oozing from those languorous eyes and taken with the incurably romantic fragrance she was wearing… She was clad in a zingy bare-midriff cocktail dress fitting her to a T – enhancing her svelte figure. We were engaged in a lip lock, my arms around her waist… Ooh la laa… She was swinging her hips provocatively as the white-hot song 'Love to love you baby' by Donna Summer played by the disc jockey bathed the environment in its erotic magic. The lights were rather dim in that crowded room – lending it a surreal atmosphere... She appeared to be a shaft of light in a whirlpool of shadows... I was hypnotized by the spell of those titillating moments and drenched in the aura of her silken charms... sinking into a state of almost disembodied bliss...floating in some sort of a private nirvana... a soporific influence impregnated the air... the gold of our hidden-elusive selves was gradually surfacing... navigating us towards uncharted waters... culminating in the never-never land... she was playfully biting my earlobes... her breath coming in hot waves... caressing my face, ears and neck... whilst huskily murmuring amorous sentiments and egging me on to live out our wildest longings in some forgotten town with a fairy-tale setting... I must have presented a pretty funny sight for I suddenly noticed my wife (who unbeknown to me had stealthily entered the room) standing in a corner visibly amused by the spectacle and appeared just a whisker away from laughing aloud. *Is reality anything but a spoil sport gnawing at most of us... If we could only substitute a make-believe world for the real world, we live in!*

Disconcerted by her presence, I promptly stopped my unimpressive, yet cathartic act and desperately tried to alleviate my bruised dignity by saying, "Don't take me that non-seriously, I used to get a big round of applause from people for a similar performance".

Bent double with an onslaught of side-splitting laughter, she raised her arms as if trying to hold onto something to stop herself from collapsing into a giggling fit again and quipped, "Don't get me wrong, my dear, but those must have been blind people!"

Good for Nothing

While informally discussing a few Civil Service Reforms introduced by the Government, a few months back, my office colleagues felt a bit unsure about a certain point. "Why not ring Anwar Khan (another colleague not present there) up and ask him about it", someone suggested.

"It's just no use", a person snapped, "actually, he is not Anwar Khan, rather he is Unaware Khan – doesn't know anything!"

Still Happy

A friend of mine, still blissfully single and endowed with a laid-back attitude towards life, recently applied for a job in the Marketing Department of a multinational. He led what could be termed as Gracious Living – marked by luxury, elegance and leisure. During the course of final interview, the Managing Director asked him, "Are you married?"

Somewhat nervous, my friend interlocked his fingers and blurted out, "No sir, I am still happy!"

The (witty) answer exploded a little later making the MD throw his head back and erupt in laughter… and he got the job.

First Date

Sometimes back, in the semi-darkness of a rainy evening, a teen-age friend of mine, susceptible to feminine charms and given to a quest for the off-beat, visited me immediately after his first date. The song 'desert moon' by Dennis DeYoung playing on the deck softly soaked the atmosphere in its soulful tune and lyrics. *Snippets from a remote past floated in a mist before my eyes.* His face was flushed with excitement and wore a 'so-in-love' expression and lambent eyes shone like twin candles of desire. *I could visualize him wooing his girl with candle-lit dinners, star-gazing sessions, roses and cards. The evening began to take on a dream-like quality… a fairy-tale aura.* I asked him how things had gone. Taking a deep breath, his face lit up like a Christmas tree as he enthused, "It was a cloud-nine experience beyond words, but what's more, it has served to improve my understanding of the theory of relativity of time".

"How interesting", I chuckled and then observed, "I could never get a handle on that theory, please do shed some educative light on it". Flattered by my receptiveness, he animatedly theorized, "Imagine a man trapped inside a hot stove, even two minutes seem like two hours to him". The point cut ice with me. I uttered, "True", and concurrently signalled an affirmative nod.

Gliding into a half-real, half-dreamy world, he added, "On the other hand, visualize a young man spending time in the company of the girl of his dreams on their first date believe (you) me, two hours pass like two minutes!"

Inch Vs A Mile

Just before leaving club after playing tombola with my friends, the other night, the parting conversation took a turn to drawing pictures of a few interesting characters known to us. The persons being talked about were Khawar and Yawar. Both professed to be playboys of some standing and insisted on being taken seriously. In our common view, the former was a live wire connecting many high-voltage romances… a sort of 'Robbing Hood' – stealing hearts of fairer sex with a keen sense of relish and luxuriating in one-night stand, while in case of latter; the term 'Playboy' appeared to be a misnomer as his gaucherie and laziness took him nowhere. No wonder that he was labelled as 'Prince of bootless errands.

Agitating the debate, I asked, "Could anyone compare the two by giving an example?" Seizing the moment, a person opined, "Well, as far as Khawar is concerned, if a girl commits the mistake of giving him an inch, he manoeuvres to make a mile of it". Chomping on his cigar and sporting a Jack-'o'-lantern smile, he continued, "Conversely, there is poor Yawar, who if a girl is stupid enough to give him a mile, might end up grabbing an inch!"

Price for Promotion

Lounged on a comfortable sofa, I kept to myself and quietly enjoyed the birthday party of my cousin's son (an eligible bachelor), who works as Manager Credits in a foreign bank and hitherto had successfully skirted the issue of his marriage. An upwardly mobile person, he believed in taking life by the reins and making the most of it. At 30, he was galvanically youthful – full of vim and verve and fond of playing clarinet. He embodied the idea of wearing the world like a loose garment and has earned the reputation of being wedded to his job.

Leading her son by hand, my cousin came and sat next to me with her son. Airing her concern, she complained, "Please advise this fellow to stop trumping up flimsy excuses of staying single and get married". After wishing him many happy returns of the day, I warmly squeezed his arm and played my ace, "Young man, it would be worth your while to know that lately I had a word with your boss about your career advancement in the bank and he gave me to understand that he could reward you with one out-of-turn promotion, provided you walk down the aisle".

In any case, I think you should work less and 'play more' and I winked while saying it.

Beaming a 100-watt smile which suffused and brightened his face, he clapped and shook his head in amusement as he jocundly remarked, "Very well, if that is the criteria for getting promotions, then I am willing to marry four times!"

Two-Timing

On one of our jaunts to a hill station, my wife spotted a married friend of mine by the name Shoaib (a playboy of the first order who changed his girls more often than his shirts and fully subscribed to the viewpoint that secret love relationships lend spice to life) walking hand in hand with a girl having a 'sex-kitten' persona – pandering to her moods – ministering to her vanities. *To abandon moral principles to please someone is – mystifying!* Exchanging sentimental softies, the insouciant lovebirds were so lost in each other that they didn't register our presence. He is like a Pied piper for girls, a Babes Bond – license to flirt. I deeply envy his rugged and unbridled individualism, boyish appeal and above all his Don-juanism – extra-marital conquests. More aptly he could be described as a romantic octopus that reached out to entwine every girl in the town with his sharp tentacles. The way the virtuoso of deception balanced his numerous love affairs involved a fair degree of dexterity comparable to a conjuror balancing a lot of balls in the air without dropping any one of them. *"Lady Luck does favour perverts too"*, I pleasurably reflected and took a long hard look at the *rainbow straddling the sky which too seemed to approve of this two-timing.*

My better (read bitter)-half who had met his wife – having a fairly plump physique, a handful of times was shocked at this brazen act of infidelity and waspishly interrogated, "This slip of a girl is not Shoaib's wife for sure, **IS SHE**?" Sidestepping this embarrassing query and dutifully protecting my friend, I tried to pooh-pooh the matter by saying, "By Jove, you are mistaken, my dear, she definitely is Shoaib's wife, only she has lost a few dozen pounds through an intensive workout course in a fitness gym".

Neither to be outdone nor so gullible, my wife gave a nasty pinch on my arm as she scoffed, "You take me for a complete fool; I wasn't born yesterday, one can only change the shape of one's body in a gym, not one's face!"

An Interesting Law

During our matriculation level, our Physics teacher followed the practice of taking a small written test after teaching a new topic to gauge our comprehension. One day when the sky was covered with ivory-coloured clouds, he explained the concept of 'Law of Heat Exchange' and then asked us to pen it on a piece of paper. Two black sheep of the class, sitting adjacent to each other, clumsily swapped their answering sheets after exchanging surreptitious glances and committed the unsavoury act of cheating.

The teacher was smart enough and caught them red-handed and demanded an immediate explanation, "What the hell is going on?" Hauling them over the coals, he jibed, "What name should I give to this shameful act?" Hot under the collar, the culprits were nonplussed and looked like hopeless lambs about to be slaughtered. One of our class fellows, given to a witty turn of phrase, defused the mounting tension and saved their skin by light-heartedly saying whilst fanning the air, "Sir, they were only practicing the Law of Sheet-Exchange!"

Hiding from Oneself

Living in a fool's paradise is sometimes one's shield from harsh reality. Recently, my unmistakably obese wife stood before the looking glass checking her make-up and over-all appearance and strangely much pleased by what she saw. Her egocentricity has propelled her to incessantly fish for compliments and toot her own horn, apparently to keep intact her shaky ego and overweening pride. An insatiable thirst for the tonic of praise all too often overthrows the monarchy of one's reason. *Much of our life is wasted in chasing trivia.* Generously pouring a subtly mesmerizing perfume on her snazzy clothes and neck, she grinned like a Cheshire cat and pouting playfully craved my attention as she conceitedly uttered, "You know what? Yesterday my best friend paid a glowing tribute to my timeless beauty by stating that I look like a rose in full bloom". After uttering these words, like a model on a catwalk, she twirled 180^0 on her heels so I could have a good look at her. *She seemed quite comfortable in the robes of a mistaken identity – adding to the glossary of deceptions.* Absorbed in desultory thoughts, I reflected on our psyche as a nation. We as a nation are playing a funny sort *of hide and seek game – hiding from truth and seeking escape from it without having the guts to face it.* **Bravo!**

Laughing up my sleeve, I pressed my lower lip between my teeth as I took a dispassionate look at the mound of flesh before my truth-seeking eyes and unwittingly pricked the bubble of her self-deception by saying, "Pardon, did I hear a cauliflower in full bloom?"

My unkind words must have hit her like a ton of bricks for she looked as black as thunder as she stormed out of the room – to hide from herself.

Politics of Desire

Becoming hostage to the politics of desire, my cousin named Altaf ventured into trying his luck for a third time on the marital wicket – seeking to make another emotional investment in a girl. By a freak of fate his earlier two marriages had dissolved. Life deals difficult cards at times. *Was he committing yet another expensive mistake?* At the nuptials, birds of a feather (married men) flocked together. The only exception was a young man aspiring to climb on the marital bandwagon. *Outdoors a raucous thunderstorm lorded it over the ceremony – punctuated only by a brief explosion of confetti and balloons, indoors. Was it another false start or a true beginning? I mused.*

The peppy bridegroom presented the picture of a powerhouse of energy... akin to an airplane revving its engine and then merrily taxiing its way to a promising take-off. His face which was beaming like a klieg light radiated a smile as warm as the sun of Sicily. He was immaculately dressed up for the occasion and could be agreeably compared to a peacock with (blue-green) feathers spread out like a fan to attract its shy mate for courtship. The incandescently alive bride had raven hair, finely sculptured face, softly radiant cheeks that switched on a cute dimple on the slightest hint of a smile, arched eye-brows and a pretty pout and beautiful iridescent blue-grey eyes – one could easily get lost in them. The wedding hall was athrob with resplendent dresses, simmering vanities, emotional fireworks… Casting a vicarious look in the direction of bridegroom, the bachelor amidst us naively remarked, "Altaf must be feeling a wee bit edgy, considering the fact that shortly he would be celebrating the first night of his wedding".

"Edgy my foot", a 50 something man mocked. (With) arms akimbo, he added, "Young man, the third time, after having known two women in the biblical sense, bridegroom is nothing but thrilled!"

Belle Époque Years

This pertains to the era, when our batch (of officers) belonging to the cadre called' Office Management Group' (an occupational group of Civil Service of Pakistan)) was undergoing its professional/departmental training programme in an Instructional Institute at Islamabad.

The hostel accommodation facility, adjacent to the Academic Block, afforded us the opportunity to spend more time together and enjoy each other's company. The stay in hostel was made all the more interesting, as fun-loving and happy-go-lucky people, who were gifted with a quick-on-the-trigger wit and many-sided humour thronged it. I may add that among such people, I am in my elements. *I still cast longing glances towards those belle époque years of my mutinous tweens – where there was a throb of expectancy in the air and the feel-good factor was present in spades. Those golden-magical moments, heady days and luminous years of youth – overflowing with the colours of freedom, adventure and idiosyncrasies are indelibly ingrained in my memory. If only one could turn the clock back and somehow reenter that glorious phase again…*

Pasted on the door of one of my sex-oriented colleagues was the message, "Sex Instructor – first lesson free". After some time, much to our amusement, someone had added to it, "All lessons free". Not wanting to be left behind in this duel of wits, another jolly-minded person, made his own contribution to the modified message stating that, "but beware, the last lesson would be charged!"

Saving Utensils

Once it so happened that my wife had gone to her parent's town and I was a grass widower. Reputed to be a gregarious fellow, during such days, my house becomes a rendezvous for friends. One day after a long hard day at office, I was completely played out and felt extremely hungry as I entered my sweet home. Invasion of kitchen (source of all eatables in our house) might have solved the problem, but being by nature prone to procrastination, I was not at all interested to clean the mass of untidy utensils, lying in every nook and corner of the kitchen. In fact, the very idea of going to the kitchen was disgusting to say the least (Yuk!) and that somewhat scaled down my appetite, making me flop down into a chair. Wanted to break the monotony and brighten the surroundings. To beat the boredom, I started strumming my guitar and singing a lively number – accompanied by sassiness of mosquitoes. *Time to drink some vodka and forget your troubles, an inner voiced beckoned. O for an isle of sanity and peace in a world of madness and tumult! Needed a meditational retreat to the Bahamas.*

At this point in time, the doorbell rang and a friend of mine – half-known, half-stranger (who had many faces and led many lives) with a cigarette dangling from the corner of his mouth ambled in through the door. "Aha", I thought, "the fly has come to the spider's web and now I will trick him into this unexciting job of dish washing". So instead of taking him to the drawing room or sitting room, I shepherded him straight to the kitchen and said the following, "Surely, you have come as a God sent angel to thoroughly wash and clean the dirty utensils".

Initially, he brushed aside the idea and immediately started talking about other things, but when I twisted his arm, he smartly evaded the menial task by saying, "I guess, you do not want your utensils to be broken!"

Settling Scores

Two of my friends as far as the art of witticism is concerned are the proverbial tit for tat. I need not say that when one is amongst them, one has to keep one's wits on high alert. During one of their visits to my place, I found them behaving like two fighter cocks and finally it slided into a slanging match.

Outside a golden summer afternoon was ebbing away... unadmired.

Stung by anger, one of them excitedly picked up a toy pistol from the side table, adjacent to the sofa set, where the other was seated. Armed with killer looks and with a glint of mischief in his eyes, he started brandishing and aiming the toy pistol at the other and sulkily cried, "How I wish this pistol were real and then all my scores would have been settled." "If that were so Mister, then naturally, I would have gotten rid of you much before you bothered to pick it up", the other riposted.

Defying Explanation

Among my acquaintances is a man, whose personality and appearance, qualify him to act without make-up in horror movies.

The other night at a stag-party thrown by him, he was recounting how during a Halloween party, his four-year old son got scared as a cornered rabbit upon beholding a man attired in Frankenstein monster's costume. Further dilating on the incident, he informed the listeners about his poor son's predicament, which according to him could be gathered from the fact that the poor lad was so much over-awed by the sight and movement of that make-believe monster that he started crying and running all over the place.

In an attempt to collect opinions, he summoned our attention and said, "I ask you gentlemen; can my son's behaviour be deemed as normal?"

"The whole episode just doesn't add up", one of his friends opined, "considering the stark reality that by virtue of residing with you, he perforce has to see you daily and by now ought to have become immune to various manifestations and faces of horror!"

Rubbing salt into host's wounds whose face wore a hurt look of stifled anguish, he heartily laughed making his eyes crinkle with hilarity and then restraining his uncouth guffaw, calmly concluded, "Well, folks, this all goes to prove a pet theory of mine that some things in life defy explanation!!"

A Marital Slice

Essaying to allure my wife out of her shell of aloofness with a view to repair our ties, which of late were a bit strained over a petty household row, I carefully struck what I reckoned to be the right note. "Queen of my captive heart, don't bottle up your emotions, let your feelings freely flow, share your concerns and above all consider me a close friend". I fancied that my silky words had knocked down the locked doors in her mind. I took a deep breath and started gazing at the aquarium placed in the left corner of the room and just beholding the gentle movement of the multi-coloured fish exercised a soothing-healing effect on me. It would be difficult to top the point made by a sage in the form of a query: Why have we chosen to become prisoners in the windowless dome of our egos? *A different world, it could be argued, cannot be built by indifferent people.*

Without preamble, my wife who wore an air of blissful unconcern and has a penchant for always having her own way intoned, "In your case, the expression 'close friend' is an oxymoron". Her words were like a twang in a melodious symphony. Jolted out of complacency,

I shuffled my feet and weakly sought clarification, "Ahem, I'm afraid; I didn't quite catch what you are driving at?"

Pausing for a while to get a load of my crestfallen look and embarrassing unease, she gracefully made her exit (bowling me over like helpless skittles) with the Parthian shot, "My dear, please understand that one can either be close to you or contrariwise be your friend!"

College Days

College life, though representing a seminal phase, has its round of carefree moments, flings of amusement and youthful follies. Beguiling flirtations, juicy gossip and some love affairs (discreet as well as open) mark campus life to a certain degree. Speaking of that time, I remember that the primary architecture of our activities was based on a sense of ridiculous, nonconformity and a spirit of adventure – often going over the edge – flirting with danger and awash in so many cross-currents of temptations. We were but slaves carrying out the biddings of our master – rushing adrenalin – goading us to break out of the quagmire of conformity. We lived life at full throttle – plotting with the devil to dismantle the reign of boring virtues. *At times life became so spicy it became difficult to digest.* The atmosphere was permeated with the scent of new beginnings and blossoming hopes.

 During my rollicking college days, I recall an evening on the tennis court of our college, where two students namely Zahid and Sameen – head over heels in love, were poised to play opposite each other. A pale autumn sunshine washed over the lawn and in its corner one could see a cat sneaking up on a rat. Before the match could start, the spectators spiritedly bucked up the lady player shouting, "Sameen, you must beat Zahid, give him a crushing defeat".

Cognizant of their well-blossomed romance, an on looker cheekily interposed, "Friends, take no pains, Zahid has already lost!"

Gains from An Accident

The other day as I was walking towards a shopping centre, I noticed a stylish young lady, wrapped up in conversation on her cell phone, whilst heedlessly proceeding to reverse her car without realizing that there was another car parked behind.

I was close enough and frantically waved my hand like a traffic cop in a bid to stop her and also raised my voice, "Watch out lady, there is a car in your way". In a flash, she glanced at me through rear-view mirror, but in her recklessness failed to halt her vehicle and resultantly it collided with the said car.

With my hackles up, I exclaimed, "Tch, tch! I tried to stop you and warned you lady, but you didn't give a hoot. Look what you've done".

A little unnerved and sheepishly looking sideways, she put a finger on her lips and huskily whispered, "*SSSHHH*... keep quiet, don't make a fuss. Here, take Rupees 5000 to cover the loss". And pronto (before I could wink) disappeared from the scene leaving me open-mouthed.

The car that got hit was not my car!

Wonderful Absence

It was a rare occasion to find myself rambling on the streets of city in the company of select friends – trying to find ourselves in the jungle of multitudinous identities and searching for meaning and stability in an upside-down world. We were all wearing wristbands named 'HOPE' – orchestrating a modest revolt against the growing menace of hopelessness. Whilst soldiering on and amidst the chaos of buses, lorries, wheel barrows, tongas, rickshaws, cars, motorcycles, pedestrians, beggars… we saw a busker doing his act in a fastidious world – surrounded by people with double standards and different faces. *The world is said to be a waystation – where we strut an hour or two. Is life on earth merely a side-show to the main event – AFTER LIFE is a question that has popped up time after time and baffled my mind.* The inclemency of a sudden downpour made us retreat into the safety of a roadside restaurant.

Enveloped in the ambience of soft background music and partaking of delicious snacks served by the restaurant, we reminisced in an unbuttoned mood about old times. After a while, imperceptibly, the conversation drifted unto marital experiences. Comparing notes and trading stories unfolded a medley of impressions ranging from pleasant to a mite unpleasant to downright bitter. By and large, most of us felt fettered by marriage, as it seemed to cramp our individuality and style and moreover did not allow us to march to the beat of our own drums. *It was hard now to stuff the genie of responsibility and cares which marriage let out, back into the bottle!*

Near our table was a picture of half-dozen cowboys in a celebratory mood having a round of drinks in a tavern as seen in a Western – manifesting the frontier spirit. This breed struts through life as if they own it. *The impulse to be somewhere else and doing something different often washed over me… filling me with a sense of unease and sadness.*

During that powwow, I noticed that one of us had kept quiet throughout as if having been drugged with silence. He sat with his legs tilted inwards and his face remained an expressionless mask. *Perhaps his mind was wrestling with some inner conflicts.* I decided to rope him in. Copying the mannerism of an interviewer, I asked him, "Daniyal, what is that you admire about your wife the most?"

Surfacing from a brown study, he tugged at his left earlobe and acidly said, "Her absence, of course!"

Seven-Year Itch

Overcome by inexplicable phenomena labelled 'seven-year itch', I found myself toying with the idea of acquiring a second wife as I sat (lost in delusions) on my rocking chair, sipping coffee and crooning, one evening in my home. The air was redolent with old longings and vague discontent. *Love and happiness are to a good life what rum and friends are to a Caribbean vacation – you cannot get in the mood without it.*

Forever suspicious, my wife, a duchess of drama and a bundle of conflicts and arguably hell-bent on stymieing my fondest wishes, intruded upon my comforting solitude with a pointed query, "What are you up to these days?" *She is someone who is in the habit of making a lot of mountains out of imaginary molehills… it surely keeps her busy.* She kept her eyes and ears open in the manner of a sleuth routinely probing beneath the surface. Fixing a smile on my face and clearing my throat, I teasingly said, "Nothing much, sweetheart, I was just weighing the consequences and wondering about your probable reaction, er, in case I were to bring a second wife in this house". I deeply relished my words and briefly looked at one of the side-walls where a lizard without a tail was chasing some insects.

Trembling with rage, she threateningly aimed a finger towards front door of the house and thundered, "The moment she would enter from that door, I shall scoot out through the back door". Her raised eye-brows seemed to touch the ceiling and her nostrils were flaring. I took a deep whiff of the scene.

"Yippee!" "It would be unbelievably sweet of you", I carolled and sent a clenched fist into the air, "but lest you later retract, let's reduce it to writing in the form of a statement signed by your gracious self".

This really took the biscuit; she was beside herself with violent anger and hollered, "You infamous scoundrel! How dare you?" and ran after me menacingly – dagger in hand…!

A Bathroom Singer

Being a passionate bathroom singer, I often drop my guard while singing during the course of taking a shower. A measure of cathartic self-indulgence does us good and somewhat assuages our inner bruises as we go along playing the hand fate had dealt us.

The other day, as I was taking a merry shower, I hammed it up and the result was a crescendo of blaring noises interspersed with bouts of off-key singing. Was I clowning to relieve some tensions? *I was bitterly reminiscing about the (many) love-affairs in my life that went sour and bemoaning my luck. Why is it so difficult to make peace with the ghosts of our lost loves? My loud voice echoed my frustration and pain as I hazily surveyed the debris of my dreams that went awry in the privacy of my bathroom... felt an almost irresistible urge to slam the door on it all and escape at least for a year into freedom.*

When I came out of the bathroom, I saw my wife standing near the bath door pressing her head. "Your singing has given me a headache". She harrumphed.

To salvage my wounded pride, I protested, "You are being unfair, I used to get a lot of clapping for such singing during my college days".

Quick as a flash, she retorted in a tone sparkling with mischief, "**Lots of clapping**, yes… *on your poor face,* **ha! ha! ha!**..."

Her unflattering remark made me raise a dissenting hand – **Oops**, making the loose towel around my waist slip down!

Spotlight On...

The two of us (my friend and I) felt a bit out of place, while attending a workshop on 'Women Rights, Problems and Challenges in the 21st century'. The next three hours unleashed a battery of high-flown sermons and over the top speeches on the given topic by ladies dressed (up) to the nines – fit to be commissioned into stardom. We would like to confess that being bored to a screaming point, we willy-nilly passed the time (that hung heavily) dozing and conveniently kept ourselves tuned out for greater part of the proceedings. **Z**zzzzz……

The luncheon after the war of words, kick-started our minds again and we managed to find seats on a round table, populated by rich and coquettish women bedecked with hefty make-up and jewellery which served as an attractive façade to conceal an ugly interior … *flashing a moneyed lifestyle. Big houses, big cars – small people!* Vanity and foolishness were writ large on their faces. *Oh my God fools have money… I should have been a fool… I would not mind being a rich fool… exercising a bit of caution with the funds… lest the fool and his money part ways.* The seductive interplay of exotic perfume scents exuded by them was flirting with our senses and their facial expressions were changing like neon-signs. The flow of conversation between the females betrayed undercurrents of jealousy, hollow pride, emotional illiteracy, superficiality and concealed rivalry – it was like an invitation to a bonfire of vanities. On the whole, we found those dissembling creatures irretrievably lost in the mist of their own conceit – wearing a mask showing outward conformity while hiding a different face underneath. My efforts to catch up with the whims of fairer sex, hitherto, have proved as futile as a caterpillar's attempt to chase a rabbit. A plastic smile clung to our faces and we gradually became quite tired of pretending to enjoy their company. "Ladies, strip yourselves of all the petty conceits and false values," I uttered half to myself which luckily remained unheard or else my head would right have been under the chopping-block. *Imagine the conversations that would take place if we actually say what we want to say rather than what is expected from us to say... then we might be left with more significant relationships or significantly fewer relationships. Most people I have realized are too full of themselves and have just closed all their positive mental faculties (if they had such to begin with).*

My friend (a master of female psychology and invested with the gift of the gab) cleverly peppered his conversation with subtle hints and (divisive) remarks calculated to play ladies off against each other. Before long, his presence brought the kind of disturbance and agitation cats cause, when let loose among pigeons.

Smelling a rat, one of them glowered at him and snarled, "Hey, don't try to sow seeds of hostility, misunderstanding and distrust amongst us sisters".

The face of the villain of the piece (my friend) creased into an easy smile as he languidly shot down the allegation, "My angry sis, as a matter of fact, I don't really need to, it has naturally been taken care of!"

Rebels Without A Cause

Our English teacher, during Bachelors level was, all in all (in our view), an eccentric person – though, no doubt, highly competent. What, however, made the situation really farcical was the fact that the students, he was supposed to educate and groom (I mean our class), excluding a few decent souls, was overwhelmingly a weird mélange of obnoxiously ill-mannered, easy-going, fun-loving and incorrigibly non-serious characters, who did next to nothing and wanted to do even less. Be that as it may, the poor instructor, picking up the gauntlet, tried his level best to iron out difficulties and chasten the unruly group through counselling, polite requests and scolding (to name just a few methods employed by him). But all his sincere entreaties and measures, sad to acknowledge, always rolled over like water off a duck's back. *Little did he realize that he was trying to grow roses in a bed of rocks. Imagine the prospects of an investor establishing a garments industry in a nudist colony or think for a moment about the naivety of a missionary preaching vegetarianism in a tribe of cannibals.*

We pursued mischief and defiance with the energy of deranged boy scouts – gaily veering away from maxims of propriety… revelling in the joys of carefree wandering… *Wow! The enviable luxury of loafing.* Our hearts had staged a coup against the democracy of manners and we were allergic to any form of dogma and platitude. Acting on impulse, we discovered, could truly put sparkle into living and we loved indulging in high jinks. Life seemed a stairway to exciting highs and swinging celebrations. One of the comical aspects of the situation included the temerity of some students to send up (that) fellow, during his spells of absence from the class – indeed a reprehensible act. A student better known in the class as 'Mr. Fatty' would sometimes in a buoyant mood, entertain us, while the teacher was away, with a belly dance, with us clapping around him – his belly sticking out and then springing back in staccato jerk, with the rhythmic movements and finesse of a master dancer. Nothing seemed off-limits.

The gentleman, eventually became (and naturally so) quite tired and frustrated with our pathetic academic performance and rambunctious conduct and one day in a fit of desperation, advised us that, "In the 3rd year final examination, he expected quality and not quantity from us". Expounding the point further, he exhorted, "Don't allow your pen to run like a racehorse, because the faster it runs, the lesser weight it carries". *If our worthy instructor's innocence were auctioned it would be worth a fortune. In examination we looked upward for inspiration, downward in desperation… Right and left for information.*

A dimwit in the class, who seemingly was only half attentive, nonsensically asked, "Sir, pardon my curiosity, but aren't we entitled to know the colour of the horse?" Before the teacher (whose face was a study in shock and disbelief) could reprimand the student for his indiscretion, the class, unfortunately, dissolved into a Niagara of clapping, senseless laughing, hooting, jeering and uncivil whistling.

This regrettably, proved to be the proverbial final straw that breaks the camel's back and our disgruntled English tutor (apparently unable to brave the nightmare anymore) went off in a huff and thenceforth (for good), left us to our lot and joined another class.

Honeymoon Days

On a trip to the kitchen during my honeymoon days, I was stunned to find my wife who was then slightly ill busy cutting the edges (both left and right by turns) of a medicinal capsule with a sharp knife. "What on earth is going on?" I almost shouted.

Blushing beet-red, she tried to soft-pedal the situation by cooing, "Oh nothing actually, don't get me wrong sweetheart, you see before taking the capsule, I was just cutting its edges to ensure that I don't suffer from its side effects".

Mirror Work

While reading newspaper one muggy evening in my home, a few months back, my eyes chanced upon my wife, who stood before the looking mirror as if transfixed. On moving closer, I found that her eyes were shut close as she faced the mirror. Strange it may seem, but it appeared as if she were staring intently at the looking glass with closed eyes.

The whole scenario piqued my interest, as I could make neither head nor tail of it and was hence constrained to inquire, "What the hell are you up to?"

Startled out of her reverie, she coyly batted her eyelashes and mellifluously said, "Nothing much, my dear hubby, I was just trying to check, how do I look like, while I am asleep".

Hair Loss

Cutting quiet waters in a paddle-boat one calm afternoon recently my wife and I were engaged in a polite, pointless chat. An on-again-off again smile was playing on her face. *She looked like she knew something about something that I knew nothing about.* Underneath us, the water of a topaz lake was lighted by oblique shafts of sunlight and spread before us like a pool of diamonds. Waved to a boy slipping pebbles across water. A sunny tranquility enfolded the place – alive with waterfowls and birdsongs. *I was frisking my moustache with the back of my hand and looked with envy at the birds that skimmed lightly across the sky and wished if I could but free myself from the baggage of old grudges and regrets and start afresh. It was time to step back and ponder my choices for a better tomorrow.* My wife (who is in the habit of keeping a close eye on me lest I transform into another being and…) aired her concern, "You are losing hair of your scalp day by day".

"My hair deficit is due to my fiscal deficit", I stammered half-jokingly as I spread my arms wide as if to hug the natural extravaganza around me.

"In that case", she jauntily remarked, "You ought to have become bald by now!"

Look Before You Leap

The other afternoon, I went to the swimming pool of Islamabad club accompanied by a rich friend of mine, who is single and very much loving it. It was a balmy summer afternoon and one could see clouds floating in cool tones of purple and lavender-grey. *I felt like opening a bottle of wine and raising a toast to a day well-spent.* Gold and flame shone in all the moving facets of water filling one with awe and a sense of poignancy about one's transient sojourn on this planet. He stood on the diving board, ready to dive. I have always admired his fun-oriented bachelorhood, buccaneering spirit and a free fall parachute like approach to life – exploring new and exciting frontiers – willing to give anything a go. It generally holds true that people who exude vitality arouse liking. His irrepressible enthusiasm, high-octane energy and infectious laugh telegraphed lively vibes, a youthful zest and a carefree independence. The roller coaster of his youth took him to dizzying heights of enjoyment and adventure. He is in the pink of health, loves the energetic pleasure of sports and leading the life of a gentleman of leisure and pleasure and seems to have wholeheartedly embraced the philosophy contained in the message: 'A bachelor is a thing of beauty and a boy forever'. *He was someone who appeared to be looking for love, but somehow always settled for making love.* Suddenly a question popped into my head and I instantly threw it at the maverick, "Hey Irteza, what's the difference between getting married and staying single?"

Cudgeling his brains for an answer, he intently gazed into the pool as if trying to delve deep beneath its surface for an elusive pearl of wisdom. Finally, he mopped his brow with his hand and evenly replied; "I guess it should be the same as between leaping without looking and looking without leaping".

After having said this, for a few seconds, he looked below and appeared a little hesitant, seemingly still cocooned in the haze of the point just made by him. Then warding off some inconsequential thoughts, he smirked and shook his head as he took a happy plunge into the refreshing pool.

Watching A Movie

It is said that a big screen makes a bad movie twice as bad. On one occasion, my two cousins and I went to see a randomly selected movie in a cinema to assess the standard of a run-of-the-mill production. To kill time, we patiently put up with a film that was by turns boring, ludicrous and atrociously vulgar. The flaccid script, unconvincing acting, weak characterization and to pile upon it the fact that there was not a ghost of a plot heightened only the agony of viewers. It would not be incorrect to say that the movie was a real torture for any normal human being. **Ho-hum!** Naturally we were exasperated to a maddening point and felt on the verge of tears. Giving vent to his growing frustration, someone from the audience shouted, "This film is the best recipe for curing chronic insomnia". Poor air conditioning in the cinema hall compounded the suffering and our state of mind beggar description. Intermission was a welcome break from the anguish we went through. Munching potato crisps and gulping down Coca cola, one of my cousins put his arm on the shoulder of other (whose marriage was on the rocks) and touched a sensitive nerve by asking, "Wasif, how is a bad movie different from a painful marriage?"

Maintaining a poker face and shaking a friendly fist at him, he dryly said, "Well, in case of a bad movie at least the misery is short-lived!"

Remembering Good Things

One Wednesday evening (22 November 2006) my wife's cousin and her husband dropped by. During the course of chitchat, the couple wished us happy wedding anniversary. This started my lachrymose wife off and wrinkling up her nose she whimpered, "Lo and behold, the unromantic and uncaring nature of my hubby could easily be judged from the fact that he has simply forgotten that today happens to be our 9th wedding anniversary, let alone, wish me". Then my snivelling wife began her litany of complaints and spoke out an Iliad of woes. *Marriage is a bit like Abstract art – hard to appreciate! Bearing tribulations with a stoic cheerfulness could be termed as an act of bravery, don't you agree?*

In a mood of reflective silence and remaining calm as a hermit in the Himalayas, my lips curled into a world-weary smile as I nonchalantly said, "My dear, one tends to remember only the good things in life!"

Short-Sightedness

It was a cloudy day as my wife and I went to drop our two children to their respective schools. Sun was battling against the conspiracy of grey-black clouds that had quite blotted it out. Breeze was crooning and rustling and blew out menacing notes. *Trees stood like lonely men – waiting for deliverance from the winds of woe. Much of my life appeared to me a series of unmerited cast backs and packed with tragedies so great that there was still a lump in my throat. Enveloped in a thick mist of disillusionments, I blearily drove on the road named 'Desolation' that seemed unending. Irked by shouldering the repertoire of conflicting identities and bedevilled with a sense of different failures, I longed to retreat from the harsh battle of life and in my mind the candle of optimism had all but sputtered out.* To dispel the demons of melancholy, I put some upbeat music on – hoping to scare away downbeat times – hankering to bid farewell to bad days for good. I was on the driving seat and scanning the weather noticed that (an insidious) fog had gradually deepened, thereby blurring the visibility of road.

I casually remarked, "The fog is so thick and pervasive that I can't see beyond 10 yards or so".

"Does it really matter?" my wife piped up as a knowing smile flickered across her face. Then giving a perfectly timed pause, she added, "Even in normal conditions, you can't see very far!"

An Exercise in Futility

Squash is perhaps the only game in which I could not improve my skills and performance though I kept on playing it intermittently over a span of few years. I remember countless evenings spent in the squash courts of Lahore Gymkhana Club, losing sometimes even to beginners. I recall an occasion, when the marker keenly observed a game I lost. In fact, my opponent had beaten me hands down. While still smarting from the defeat as I stood in the squash court, I found myself asking him about my ranking amongst the current lot of players.

Above in the sky a listless moon presided over an unjust world.

Reflecting for a moment, he plainly answered that I stood at 100th number.

His words were a jab to the pit of my stomach. Raising my left arm over a woebegone face and rolling my eyes heavenward I protested, "Wait a minute, only yesterday you told me that presently only 42 players are enlisted here". "Then how come my ranking is below 42?" I demanded as I strove to salvage my pride from the debris of accumulated disappointments. *Complexes, inhibitions and failures are heavy baggage to carry.*

"A good question". He acknowledged and a friendly smile flitted across his face as he explained, "Please don't take offence, having seen your game from time to time, I am inclined to believe that the overwhelming majority of players joining in the future are likely to be better than you!"

It was one of the sincerest and unforgettable compliments I have ever received.

Some Tidbits

(i) Two friends, Mateen and Omar were discussing their common friend Sohail, when Mateen remarked: "Sohail has a mechanical bent of mind, but how unfortunate that some of the screws are loose".

"No", added Omar, "Some are tight!"

(ii) Teacher to his class: "Give me a practical example of taking a joke seriously?"

A student: "A sober and sane woman marrying a jester".

(iii) Two close friends, Akbar and Rasheed were treating themselves to a lively chat over a cup of tea one evening and the topic of discussion was their marriage plans. Suddenly Akbar asked Rasheed, "Frankly speaking, what is your idea of a perfect wife?"

Ruminating over it for a while, Rasheed replied, "Well, a girl who is beautiful, educated, brainy and homely would fit the bill."

Sporting a high-beam grin, Akbar commented, "Why don't you come straight to the point and say that you want to marry four girls".

(iv) Two colleagues, Aamir and Talat were having lunch in the office canteen. Aamir aired an opinion about their boss, "Don't you agree that our boss is quite a gentleman and polished?"

"But the trouble is", Talat sarcastically interjected, "that he is only gentle from far and for the polish, well, it is confined only to his shoes".

(v) Young man: "Am I not the loving prince of your dreams?" "Do you not", he continued, "Dream about me sometimes?"

Girl: No, as a matter of fact, I am not fond of nightmares.

(vi) A comment about a licentious and decadent man, "He was not allowed to board the plane as it could not carry the weight of his dirty thoughts.

(vii) A comment about a girl, "Her loose clothes are not the only loose thing about her".

(viii) A comment about the paper-setters of examinations, "They ask you the wrong questions, but you have to give the right answers".

ix) Height of Lawlessness: Act of snatching a car at gunpoint by robbers while riding on a car already snatched by them.

x) Daughter: Daddy you shouldn't smoke, otherwise you will disappear (in smoke) one day.

xi) Choosing a career: Wanted to become a gangster and a preacher. Father refused me both… so ended up becoming a teacher.

xii) Guilty or not? If I've rented out my house... am I guilty of rent-seeking behavior?

xiii) Students' blues before exams: "Nothing is going as planned. Nothing! Ironically the plan to not study at all is the only plan that goes according to the plan!"

xiv) Lawyerly look at Santa Claus: 'Only once a year' visit is the clause that comes with Santa.

xv) Life is a garden and girlfriends are the flowers... and he is a butterfly who wants to sit on every flower.

Second Cup of Tea

In a high-tea party thrown by one of my friends to celebrate the first birthday of his son, I was among the Johnny-come-lately. When I reached, the party was more than halfway through and presented a convivial atmosphere. The guests were chatting and enjoying to the hilt the delicious and mouth-watering snacks with obvious relish. Tea was also being served and the guests throwing all formalities aside were sniffing and slurping it and praised to the high heavens its good taste and aroma.

Smacking my lips in (delicious) anticipation I hastened towards the snacks and tea. Yum-yum! At this point in time, my friend's wife, a graduate from the school of charm, acting as a hostess and who did not notice that I had just arrived, sauntered through the busy crowd and came close to me. *She had a Venus-like visage with a movie-star appeal – setting many a heart aflutter!! Her charming modesty, an understated elegance, dulcet voice, wide-set hazel eyes and a beautiful, golden-girlish laughter attracted men like moths to a flame. Her eyes were so deep that I felt one could fall into them and never reach the bottom. Whenever, she entered a room (or an open space) everyone would momentarily drop whatever they were doing, turning their eyes towards her – she had such a magnetic-alluring presence. If wives were made to order, one would have ordered someone like her.* In the lawn, a little distance behind her, I could see fireflies blinking and twinkling through the trees under a gibbous moon.

She was attired in a pomegranate red dress that meshed perfectly with her glistening rosy cheeks – that appeared to have just been artistically kissed by freshness of morning dew. Her dazzling beauty, impeccable sartorial grace and panache enamoured the invitees and one felt rich by her golden glance. Phrased another way, she looked like thistledown wafting in a world of dreams. Kohl had accentuated the size of her eyes, giving them a lustrous appearance. Her black hair fell softly across her shoulders. Que bella! Tipping my hat with a relaxed smile, I bowed and kissed her outstretched hand. Clad in a disarming smile, she in turn placed her hand on my arm and in a soft resonant voice suggested, "Kamran, how about a second cup of tea?" *One brief moment, I drank in that soul-ensnaring glance and felt helplessly entangled in her kiss-curl. If only one could live in an intoxicating dream world… taking a draught of reality, every now and then…*

In a voice that must have conveyed more foolishness than innocence and with my arms outstretched in a questioning manner and my brows knit, I protested, "But I did not have the first one!"

Lust at First Sight...

One of my friends is a four-square admirer of female pulchritude. He is a puppet in the hands of a sybaritic lifestyle – wallowing in dissipation and debauchery as if there was no tomorrow. He loved the playfulness of life and did not mind venturing out into unmapped and stimulating realms of human experience. *It takes courage to tread your own path rather than following the one culturally carved for you. Meanderings, wanderings and detours... teach us a lot, taking us through the journey.* On one occasion when the sky was embellished with cognac-coloured clouds, the two of us got a wonderful opportunity to attend a 'Bikini Contest' held on a beach in Hawaii, USA. The fact that the participants of the pageant wore mini bikinis, leaving little to imagination was an icing on the cake and the excited spectators clamoured for more whilst quaffing champagne and swigging beer bottles. The contenders proved to be matches, successively sparking the tinderbox of sexual passion... sending the adrenalin coursing through our veins. Our fingers were on the trigger of desire as we exchanged hidden glances and occasional winks with one another – enjoying moments of irresponsible leisure – trying to make the most of this no-strings attached time. *Untutored eyes gel well with an untutored mind and heart!*

One of the contestants with ravishing good looks, cuddlesome curves, blazing blue eyes and oomph became the cynosure of all eyes and made the onlookers gasp in admiration. She was attired in a vibrant (flame) orange bikini with a view to consume others with passion and lust. She was armed with a breathtaking figure and a bust, which could have arguably put Mae West on the back foot. Her flirty, sexy and naughty way of walking was a tantalizing choreography that could have made even the anchorites swoon with delight and succumb to the desire of copulation with her. She had a body that could have tempted a priest. She was in other words, a visual feast for hungry eyes and a true sensual persuader. She strutted as a bouncy, luscious and figure-flaunting siren that made the male onlookers whistle wolfishly and cheer out of sheer admiration. Her devilishly attractive features, come-hither looks, burning sidelong glances, flirting hips and wanton smile provided enough fodder for our salacious minds – inducing us to commit moral hara-kiri at the altar of temptation. *The lure of the forbidden is hard to resist!* The slave of desire (read me) felt like kneeling in supplication before this Countess of sex-appeal. The air was thick with sexual heat driving out shyness, modesty and restraint as the devil of hot desire got the better of the effervescent male lot and they got carried away – *adrift in a sea of folly.*

My friend stood stock-still and utterly spellbound and his gaze was transfixed – beholding her mind-blowing hooters, which were like two hillocks of loveliness proudly jutting out to conquer the world. 'Princess Erotic' as we called her was in every sense, a true acme of female beauty. *If I told her that she had a beautiful body. Will she hold it against me? I wondered.* Shamelessly relishing the heady wine of her waist-up charms, my friend took a long pull at the bottle and pumping up his fist in the air cried, "Jesus (Christ)! I like this girl!". "And the reasons are quite obvious" I laughingly added.

Unnecessary Demand

While hanging about a market recently, my (maximalist) wife drew my attention to a stall selling face-masks of different animals presenting fairly savage moods.

The face-mask of a wolf caught her fancy. She excitedly picked it up and implored, "Please buy me this one!"

Snorting with laughter, I angled my head at her and wryly said, "I don't think you really need one!"

Clinging to Youth

Believing oneself to be younger than one's biological age is nothing but natural and a pardonable weakness. Not long ago, a cousin of mine, shy of his 60th birthday by two months, underwent an eye-surgery. Shortly afterwards, at a grand family get together, he came wearing pitch-black glasses (possibly on doctor's advice to shield eyes from light) that meshed well with a (salt and pepper) walrus moustache and a matching goatee occupying the lower parts of his gaunt face that could no longer defy the ravages of time. My eldest paternal uncle, a sprightly 84 years old, endowed with the ability to steal the show primarily on account of his jolly disposition, an impromptu humour and knack for repartee, greeted him in a lively manner by affectionately patting his back and jovially saying, "How are you doing young man?"

Visibly flattered by the comment, my cousin modestly replied that he was doing about fine and started to explain the condition of his eyes. Just then, panning his eyes around the room, my uncle quickly took in the guests present on the occasion and playfully put in, "Look, he hasn't denied that he isn't young!"

An Emotional Punching Bag

To stir the dying embers of enthusiasm and to perk up my mood, I was dancing to the beat of fast music in the privacy of my room, the other evening. My wife slunk into the room and started clapping and cheering. After finishing the act, I respectfully placed my left hand on my stomach and bowed low and thanked her for being appreciative. I felt an inward flutter of delight. An ingratiating smile played around the corners of my mouth. Spreading an evil grin over her face, she critically said, "It's quite sensible of you to confine your dancing to the privacy of your room and not doing it publicly".

To counter the point made by her and also bolstering my sinking ego, I told her that almost 25 years ago I gave a solo dance performance during one of the wedding functions of a close friend of mine. "You know what?" I excitedly said, "the people gathered on that occasion were so strongly affected that all of them stood up in the middle of my performance and then…"

Before I could complete the sentence my wife promptly interrupted me and said, "… and then understandably they ran away – they could hardly be blamed!!"

Having said that she laughed loudly to her heart's content and then taking cognizance of my simmering rage took to her heels.

And I was left alone to angrily shower punches on the poor punch bag that hung in the corner of the room – more used by me as an emotional punching-bag.

A Movable Asset

Lately I visited my bank and noticed a new man behind the cash counter and upon inquiry it transpired that it was a routine interbank transfer. Interestingly, his predecessor was quite unpopular on account of a 'couldn't-care-less' stance toward colleagues and work.

Spoiling for a little fun, I made a tongue-in-cheek remark to his supervisor with whom I had a nodding acquaintance. Faking a smile, I averred, "The transfer of your ex-teller is a big loss". "He was indeed", driving the point home I emphasized, "an invaluable asset for the bank".

Staring at me in a state of amused disbelief, he comically shot back, "An asset, oh yes", he grinned, "but thank God a movable one!"

Think Tank

As Civil Servants, we are required to attend short-term refresher courses from time to time, meant for capacity building of government functionaries by building on their job-related skills and knowledge. Recently, I happened to attend one such course titled, "Management theories and practices". During the currency of the course, one of the instructors was angling for an apt definition of term, 'Think-Tank' and encouraged the participants to come up with their own understanding of the concept.

Many good definitions were tossed to and fro, but the most interesting and apparently an original one coined went like: Think Tank, "Thinking done, while sitting in a tank".

What Are Wives For…

While watching a bevy of lissome models doing catwalk on a T.V channel recently, I casually remarked, "I've noticed that most of the models and film heroines are quite slim – physically they haven't got much to offer – I wish they were pleasantly plump".

"If you are that fond of fatness and it turns you on", my strapping wife said in an excited tone, "then I'm right here for you, my sweetheart", and gave me such a bear's hug that left me gasping for breath.

Match-Making

I have a female cousin, who has a thirty-four years old (beanpole) son, given to a bohemian lifestyle, quicksilver temperament, recalcitrant attitude, off-putting manners and darker pastimes. His bushy eye-brows, chunky moustache, squinty eyes and a scrubby beard gave him an air of ruffianism. His appearance during (his) waking hours could be described as **'from bed to worse'** and he is as unsociable as a bear. He was someone who acknowledged his demons, but did little to rein them in. The larrikin in question has been shirking from marriage on one pretext or another. Having a soft spot for this oddball, I took it upon myself to put his life on a worthwhile track.

During a tête-à-tête with my cousin in the lawn of her house (ablaze with flowers) lately, I was probably sticking my oar in, when I said, "A will-o' the wisp like your son, immediately needs to be brought within the fold of marriage to tame and bridle his waywardness and devil-may-care attitude". Steering the point further, I philosophized, "I am sure you would agree that marriage is likely to exercise a stabilizing influence on him, buoy up his self-image and if you evince some interest, I have a few fine girls in mind, who could be considered for tying the knot". Having said that, I expectedly looked towards her for a word of appreciation for my solicitude and more importantly awaited her response to my proposal as I sat inhaling refreshing spring air. The retiring sun was casting long shadows and we could hear birds squabbling noisily. A rose-purple glow slowly deepened on the sky. I could spot some ducks grazing on the front lawn.

Abstracted in a maze of thoughts, as if trying to put pieces of a frustrating puzzle together, she gave a mirthless smile, briefly looked at her pet cat that was snoozing in the chair next to her and tartly said, "Dear cousin, do you have some kind of an old enmity with those pitiable girls?" And then she suddenly broke into Woody Woodpecker's five-note wacky laugh.

With egg on my face and wits all but tattered, I tried to raise my voice in protest, but she did not allow me to get a word in edgewise and narrowing her eyes almost to slits delivered the finale, "You appear to be covertly scheming, to get even with at least one of them, through this ill-fated matchmaking!"

Escaping From…

After dropping his children to school and before going to office, my younger brother manages to steal 20 minutes or so daily for a brisk walk or jog in a park before leaving for office. Generally pressed for time, he often goes into an overdrive and could be seen running all over the place in a bid to hastily finish his drill of morning exercise.

Over the course of a recent get together of our cousins who had gathered for a wedding ceremony, a female cousin of mine (who also regularly visits the same park for a walk in the morning which is frequented by my brother) upon meeting my brother lightly remarked, "I see you daily in that park and you appear to be in such a state of terrible hurry that it seems you are trying to outrun something". Then after a pause she laughingly inquired, "What exactly are you trying to run away from?"

"From his circumstances", my youngest brother who was listening to this conversation piped up.

Mother's Day

On 'Mother's Day' my elder son who is in his early teens and seems to have a degree in naughtiness was in a quiet-gentle mood and softly said, "Mom you told me that angels are in heaven. If it's true, then what are you doing here?"

"Looking after the devil!" my younger daughter promptly replied whilst lifting a hand in a mock salute.

One Down and Nine to Go!

Many years ago, at a fashion show organized in the auditorium of our college, the models' catwalk attracted lascivious looks and tumultuous applause from the male students, who were through and through entranced by the wavy, sensuous and titillating gait of enchanting models attired in flamboyant clothes and eye-catching designs. Their figure-flattering dresses were a medley of colours – salmon pink, lemon bright, deep jungle green, thunder-cloud grey, tempest-blue, cherry red, lily-white and flame-orange just to mention a few notes. They appeared like a bevy of exotic birds on a charm offensive – proudly displaying their colourful feathers as they sashayed down the catwalk and gave each other a good run for their money.

Males (essentially hedonistic creatures) were having a helluva good time and blew kisses across their open palms and whistled like roadside loafers, much to the chagrin of our ten female class fellows, who were green with jealousy and fretted inwardly at our lust-laden eyes and felt (rightly so) they were being an encumbrance to us. The fact that the flashy dolls had captivated our (sin-prone) minds in the manner of a hypnotist and that we had become oblivious to their very presence was nothing less than a slap in their faces. We exulted over their discomfiture and to capture the moments took snapshots. The vampish glamour of the atmosphere jiggled our lecherous hearts with its voluptuous tunes and we went berserk. *Alas, the charade of our decency fell apart like a house of cards before the tempest of our animal impulses. In retrospect, I wonder and am often left intrigued while recollecting how our mercurial lives and vagabonding tendencies were further swept by the turbulent tides of an untamed youth and how it prompted us to repeatedly crash against the embankments of an insipid status quo.* **Good old days! Where did those days vanish??**

Taking exception to our base sensibilities and carnal fixation, one of them raised a deprecating hand and rebuked, "***Phew!*** We are sick and tired of being labelled as mere sex objects".

Scoring her off, a sharp-tongued boy of the same class flashing a roguish grin whilst jabbing his finger at her teasingly said, "You don't understand, my little simpleton, you are supposed to be sex objects. What are you, if not sex objects?"

Hearing this, the po-faced girl went crimson with shame and hot blushes, clenched her fists and left the scene on the wings of embarrassment.

"That's one down and nine to go!" he gloated over his first victory making a thumbs down sign whilst sticking out his tongue.

Being Oneself

Every Sunday before noontime, I go to Vegetable-cum-Fruit Bazaar (called 'Sunday Bazaar') to buy a week's supply. The said bazaar is heavily crowded throughout that day, because compared to market; their rates are relatively wallet-friendly.

I normally take my shower and breakfast after coming back from that bazaar. During my last trip there, I bumped into a friend of mine who was carrying in both hands vegetable and fruit items and looked dishevelled and weary – sweating as in a sauna. Upon meeting me, he excused about his unwashed face and untidy appearance and in a defensive tone assured me that he would take his morning shower as soon as he reached home. Draping a comforting arm around his shoulders, I said, "My friend relax, go easy on yourself and don't feel guilty at all on that account". Then inviting his attention to my own unkempt appearance, I added, "Look at me, I too am in the same untidy state and like you would get fresh on reaching back home".

Smiling crookedly with one side of his mouth whilst scanning me from head to foot with an X-ray like gaze, he abrasively said,

"Frankly, I have never noticed any difference in your appearance (at other times also)!"

Ransom for Handsome

Seeking a few moments' respite from the treadmill of office routine, we gathered the other day, in one of our colleague's office for some refreshments and chit-chat. Incidentally that day's newspaper was aswarm with news items on 'kidnappings' that had occurred in various parts of the country. Law and order seemed to have gone on a jolly long holiday. I could spot dust hanging in the shafts of sunlight in his room.

After voicing his concern and condemning such dastardly acts, our host colleague started staring intently at a painting hung on one of the walls of his office that masterly depicted a ship trying to brave a relentless sea-storm in its bid to stay afloat. *Are we in the thick of a nightmare having the appearance of a reality or was it vice versa?*

To break the silence and for the sake of fun, one of us asked him, "What would your wife do if you get kidnapped for ransom?"

Wearing a self-deprecating smile, he replied, "She would definitely pay the ransom", then pursing his lips continued, "on the condition that the kidnappers take the ransom and keep me too!"

You Too…

When one of my worldly-minded friends, better known by his surname Usmani (given to a sinful and decadent lifestyle) came back after performing the holy pilgrimage (Hajj), which has been enjoined by our religion (Islam), we held a dinner in his honour. At the get together that took place in one of our common friend's house, we allowed him to take the maximum lead in conversation.

With a cinematic eye, he graphically recalled the various rites and stages of pilgrimage and his state of mind and sentiments during their performance. He particularly got emotional in describing a ritual carried out at a place called Mina (which is on the outskirts of Mecca). At that place, muslim pilgrims (in flocks) lapidate two hillocks believed to be the personifications of devil. This is done to curse the devil, express hatred and condemnation for his handiworks and reaffirm one's faith, loyalty and love to Allah (Almighty). Put another way, it underscores that believers pelting stones at those manifestations of fiend are not part of his party, but are on the opposite side of the divide under God's tutelage.

Reliving that incident, he got so overcome by a spiritual trance that his voice repeatedly trailed off three to four times and he just couldn't complete the sentence. He kept on uttering, "When I passionately threw stones at the two hillocks, I .... (Repeat). *Devil has many guises and disciples too!*

Quickly picking up the thread of that unfinished sentence, one our friends who had been listening to the whole account with rapt attention and has a knack for sparkling wit (*that gets uncorked at the drop of a hat*), chipped in and grinning from ear to ear wickedly said, "Immediately after throwing stones, you must have heard the wail of anguish issuing from Satan... pitiably crying, "***You too, Usmani!***"

The Unfaithful H...

Occasionally I give to my wife (who is more complicated and challenging than a 36 across and 14 down major crossword puzzle and never passes up a chance to take potshots at me) a thumbnail account of some interesting incidents taking place during the hurly burly of office hours. The other afternoon, riding the high horse of over-confidence and feeling as proud as Lucifer, I told my wife about my recently posted boss, who from my appearance was under the impression (which he conveyed) that I must be a newly inducted member of Pakistani Civil Service.

"I can imagine". She brightly interposed arching an eyebrow in a faux-seductive manner.

"I was honest enough to inform him that I was 45 years old and had more than 21 years of public service to my credit." I recalled.

"Go on dear". She encouragingly said tapping the end of the ballpoint on her chin. There was a sparkle of coruscating mischief in those charcoal eyes adorning a mobile face.

"He expressed his surprise by roundly stating that I looked far younger and that my boyish features betrayed an age somewhere between mid-to-late thirties". Repeating those words before my fastidious wife was soothing music to my praise-starved ears and I felt like a celebrity basking in the afterglow of a well-deserved compliment and in an elated mood declared, "*Yay!* Three cheers for my truly great boss". "The cap definitely fits, what do you say, eh?" I looked at her squarely in the eye, seeking unqualified support.

"His eyesight, I am afraid appears to be quite weak and for his own good sake, you ought to advise him to immediately seek help of a good ophthalmic optician to rectify the faulty vision leading to inexcusable judgement, lest it's too late and he suffers". She spoke as usual straight from the shoulder. Her eyes were snapping and flashing with a wicked glee.

My face fell to my toes. Each word was like a hammer blow making successive dents in the protective shell of my masculine pride. *She draws a wicked pleasure from needling me and hiking my woes, a judgemental inner voice pricked and I got buried in the quicksand of self-pity.* "Hmmm, what'll happen if he doesn't and carries on?" I tepidly whined whilst drumming my fingers on the table and started fantasizing about leading a carefree existence in a dream house on a mountain top. *Sadly, the life we want to live is the life most of us would never be able to lead!*

Allowing herself a foxy smile, she pertly said, "Then naturally his eyes would keep on playing such stupid tricks on him and he might end up becoming a model laughing stock".

Locking a pair of expressive eyes with me and twining her arms around my neck, she delivered the coda of her sermon: "By the same token, ready credulity, my easy-to-please hubby, should not be included in the curriculum of your beliefs".

And, alas, I fell flat on my face from the unfaithful h….

A Minor Operation

Economic Affairs Division, where I was employed in the year 2004 has an officers' mess that caters for social needs of employees and serves as a rendezvous for weekly get-together. It helps people in taking things easy for a while, and to enjoy each other's company, over a cup of tea and snacks.

During one such session, we were engaged in badinage. One of our colleagues, who was then in charge of the mess, introduced a friend of his, a doctor by profession and mentioned that he recently benefited from his services in getting rid of his conscience through an operation.

We were reduced to laughter, the moment a colleague bantered, "I can bet, it must have been a very minor operation".

Robbed Of...

Before going to an official reception, I was checking my over-all appearance. I was particularly pleased by my glowing face on which I had just applied a cleansing lotion. Entirely satisfied by my looks, I gave an admiring nod to my reflection in the mirror. I was about to turn away from the wall-sized mirror, when my spouse pricked the bubble of my vanity by cruelly saying, "Don't you get scared by looking at yourself in the mirror!"

And I felt as a tramp robbed of his scanty belongings.

Homework Blues

Recently while explaining to my daughter (Saliha) the meaning of the word 'handsome' which was part of her English-subject homework, I light-heartedly remarked that, "During the days of his prime youth, people used to call your pa handsome". Hearing this, my daughter seemed pretty impressed. I gave a burp of contentment and rubbed my hands in self-congrat.

Sporting a whiplashing smile, my wife who was privy to this talk promptly crushed my burgeoning pride by saying, "Saliha, let me inform you that all the people who used to call your pa handsome, later underwent eye operations".

Appearances Could Be...

One evening, all alone on the roof terrace, I was amusing myself by loudly singing a latest Indian hit song. To give high-voltage effect to the song, I imitated the passionate singing style and body language of a pop-singer performing live and reacting to a highly charged audience. My actions could be compared to that of a fountain gone crazy – sometimes you ought to go haywire. *I was desperately trying to pull myself out of a quagmire of depression. For a long time in my life, good luck had been quite conspicuous by its very absence and I felt like running away for good – from myself. When I look back, I don't forgive myself for a lot of things. Visualized myself as a rudderless ship headed for the sharp rocks. A miasma of sadness and fatigue enveloped me and I was as if stranded in a deep well of loneliness and helplessness – climbing out of which was becoming exceedingly difficult with each passing day. How long can one drink the cup of bitter grief and still pretend to be happy? Can one face up to a relentless onslaught of enervating disappointments and set-backs (one after another without any let-up) and still not run out of steam and give in to despondency? How very painful it is – clinging to the sinking raft of one's hopes? How long life could be put on hold? The summer of my discontent was heating up…*

Out of nowhere my wife appeared on the scene and after raising a questioning brow tauntingly inquired, "**Good Grief!** Are you singing or trying to scare?"

My Name Is Not...

The pigeon-pair, my (elder) son and (younger) daughter are as different as chalk and cheese and often end up fighting with each other while playing together. My son has a flaming temperament that gets ignited at the drop of a hat. His irascibility coupled with rapidly swinging moods has made him a real handful. Conversely, my daughter is soft-spoken, low-key and blessed with an equable disposition. Confrontation is not in her playbook. On a contentious point, the other evening, my son hit the roof and lashed out at his sister, "Are you mad?"

Calm as a pond, my daughter innocuously said, "My name is not mad."

Prices and Wives Are

~~~~~ॐ~~~~~

Lately a friend of mine accompanied by his wife visited with us. During the round of a light-hearted conversation – we filled each other in on some interesting news and spicy gossip; I finally navigated towards one of my hobby-horses viz the ever-looming challenge of a constant increase in the over-all cost of living and the disquieting impact of a relentless price-hike encompassing almost all consumer products. To substantiate my point, I said, "These days my son is pestering me to buy him an indoor video game system called 'Play Station' and imagine its latest edition 'Play Station 3' costs a cool Rs 53000". Having said that I heaved a resigned sigh and pulling a long face added, "I've become weary of the growing ascendancy of a soulless materialism which has rendered it next to impossible to keep up appearances and I wish prices of products were more wallet-friendly". *Truth has become such a cheap commodity nowadays, yet it is in short supply! Strange economics seems to be ruling the roost. What is the world coming to?*

Hearing my grievance, my friend focused his (forgiving) eyes on his wife who was sitting at a pistol's shot from him and jestingly remarked, **"My friend always remember that prices and wives are seldom friendly!"**

A Courteous Nation

During my visit to the Land of Rising Sun (Japan), I was pleasantly surprised to observe the elaborate courtesy, humility and gracious comportment exhibited by Japanese people. Concern for others is an attitude that is inbred, nurtured and developed throughout their lives. Similarly, sensitivity to others' feelings is also deeply embedded in their psyche. These impressions were further reinforced, when I happened to witness first-hand a collision between two cars on a busy road in Tokyo. The two Japanese gentlemen calmly parked their vehicles on a side lane and strolled towards each other.

Upon coming closer, one of them bowed low and politely said, "Sorry, it was my fault". Much to my surprise, the other person followed suit by taking a quick bow and apologetically saying, "No sir, it wasn't your mistake, I was at fault".

Then the two decent men shook hands, wished each other a good day and parted.

The Moon Needs A…

Many years ago, while playing in the garden of our house, my eight-year-old son looked towards the clear star-studded sky and after scanning it mumbled to himself, "I don't see the moon, I am missing its company and wonder where it has gone?"

His younger sister nearly five years of age within earshot, matter-of-factly said, "You stupid, don't you know that tonight the moon is on a holiday".

Kingdom of Darkness

Sometime back, a friend of mine (a voluptuary by temperament who led life according to the teachings of his prodigal heart), still innocent of wife, threw a housewarming reception where couples were invited for merrymaking – unfolding a 'no-holds-barred' type of evening. In two shakes of a lamb's tail, the party was swarming with life like a beehive. The guests kept rhythm with the rip-roaring celebrations and appeared like pilgrims astray in a mecca of temptations – blending well with the vibes of a cognac-drenched night. Females emitted short sharp shocks in the darkness like impetuous lightning bugs – giddy with delight as they cruised headlong on a voyage of self-discovery – raring to fling themselves into the arms of life. Booze was flowing freely and air began to crackle with music and sheer physical energy. Cut loose from usual inhibitions, the revellers presented a mosaic of movement, colours and reckless abandon – that took them out of themselves. The strobe light showed a couple snogging in a corner flanked by some teenagers who were sniffing cocaine to get a few moments high. My eyes zoomed in on a sassy girl wearing a champagne-coloured dress saying something to a hunky young man with her right hand cupped over his ears. All over the place, couples could be seen dancing cheek-to-cheek and exchanging kisses and loving whispers. The unforgettable number 'I feel love' by Donna Summer playing on the deck regaled the hearts of guests with its simmering spell. Everybody was tanked up, danced their blues away and had a gorgeous time. A happy haze stole over a stupor-driven night – that seemed blacker than a devil's heart and a delicious drowsiness swam in the liquid eyes of party creatures as they jettisoned their grief into the well of momentary forgetfulness. *Drink to make the world go away or drink to create another world that you love.*

"*What a relief that would be if only we could keep the load of worldly worries off our chests for good and rescue our dreams from becoming pliant hostages to the whims of a sadist fate. Sanity is difficult to lose, but equally hard to keep.*" I pensively wondered while floating in and out of a dreamy state induced by four stiff pegs of whiskey... *playing back in my mind a fading cavalcade of people and places... I seemed to be moving in a dream...* One is usually in an expansive mood after a good drink. *The air was pregnant with vague yearnings and unfulfilled dreams and a sense of longing with an inability to designate what was longed for. Will we ever be able to tie up the loose ends of our lives? Hasn't the world started resembling a market abounding with sorrows and troubles where fruits of joy and calm had become rare-precious commodities – not within the reach of a vast majority? Is there any light at the end of the tunnel?*

One of the invitees, a married man, a fervent advocate of the merits and blessings of marriage and openly critical of people shying away from it, while nursing his drink proposed a toast, "Staying unmarried is sign of a misspent youth".

Not rising to the bait, the tipsy host with a mask of paint on his face, dissolved into a belly-laugh – naughty as strip tease, lifted his wine-filled glass up and slurred, "Hey, c'mon, my friends, don't buy this piece of malarkey, in fact, truth is precisely the opposite – remaining single is mark of a well spent youth!" There was a sensual languor in those wine-dimmed eyes as he raised his glass and said: "To the joy of living".

Above in the sky, a tired moon sporadically took refuge in the understanding clouds and the two wanderers appeared to be scheming to perpetuate the kingdom of darkness!

A Monk in the Making

For a few days after my engagement, I felt like a fish frolicking happily in the waves. This joy and thrill, however, proved to be short-lived. Soon I found myself wrestling with my (hard to repress) freewheeling bachelor instincts that have often led me astray, mostly landed me in trouble and goaded me to explore yet greener pastures of new experiences. With ring round my finger and shackles around my heart and mind, I thought of myself as a Samson with his locks shorn – engagement started looking like containment. *I felt as a ship – trapped in a bottle! Or picture a man with a chalice of sparkling-tantalizing wine placed in front of him, but who alas has been chained to a post thereby thwarting him from reaching and savouring it.*

One fine evening (a month or thereabouts after my engagement), when the sky was overcast with blue-black wispy clouds – a chum of mine (hitherto unengaged and very much a free soul) picked me up from my home and we ostensibly went jogging to a popular park. His credo – Live "in-the-here-and-now" has always impressed me. The chirping of the birds combined with the sounds, sights and smells of spring made us feel relaxed as we roamed amidst the riot of colours that looked vibrant as trumpets. To onlookers, we must have appeared like two carefree puppies sniffing around to see what was new – pining for some fun and adventure – yearning to catch up with life. The congenial environment of the park liberated us from the intertwining webs of our mundane worries and soon we felt free as birds riding air currents.

Upon beholding two traffic-stoppingly beautiful girls, I got so carried away that I started jogging backwards to keep pace (with) and not lose sight of them for a single moment. After jogging in this manner for a while, I clumsily bumped against another person and was about to fly off the handle, when upon quickly turning around, the sight of the person, first made me hold my horses and then took my breath away and in a jiffy my heart started pounding like a steam engine – **da-dum**, *da-dum*, **da-dum**… I just couldn't believe my traitorous eyes and bit my finger, for right in front of me (believe it or not) stood my brother-in-law (my fiancée's brother who incidentally also happened to be a good friend of mine) who had caught me on the wrong foot. I was nonplussed or to be more exact you could say so thunderstruck that for an instant, I did not know whether I was standing on my head or on my toes – you could have easily knocked me down with a feather. One had to be blind not to see the guilt and shame written in big block letters on my face as I desperately sought a credible excuse to downplay the whole episode.

Reading the situation, my brother-in-law bitingly observed, "***Whew!*** If I remember correctly, you are the same person, who recently got engaged to my sister and I must say that these sort of irresponsible teenage antics and boyish capers do not behove you anymore". Holding my ground, I promptly defended my position and histrionically replied, "Granted, I am engaged, but that doesn't mean that I have become a complete monk!"

Perhaps the (clownish) way, in which I framed my words, somehow took the edge off the tense situation and we ended up laughing loudly and giving each other five.

Food for Thought

After having drawn a balance sheet of gains and losses, accruing from a variety of dietary choices and eating habits, I was out and out convinced of the overriding benefits of foods taken in their simplest forms like baked or boiled, so as not to compromise their inherent nutritional value. This point of view was based on my perusal of standard articles, providing dietary tips on healthful living. I was so much swayed by the persuasive appeal of this fantastic idea that I decided to introduce it into my household forthwith. At (the) first blush, the notion seemed feasible. I may add here that this decision immediately brought within me a sense of euphoria and jauntiness and I felt drunk with optimism and began staring out of the window – lost in daydreams… O; for a vacation home on a shimmering lakeside surrounded by cherry trees and enfolded in a somnolent serenity – offering an idyllic existence… where I could proceed on a holiday of undisturbed contemplation – in search of deeper and truer insights and uncharted horizons to change the course of my life…

Digressing a little, it ought to be mentioned that my family (a wife and two children) is a diehard devotee of fried food, served with loads of chillies, spices and gravy. Selling the idea (under reference) to such diametrically different people and getting them round to my viewpoint, which demanded a U-turn in their eating preferences would be akin to a Herculean task, I mused.

However, (keeping) a stiff upper lip, I decided one evening to tackle the problem head-on. My family at that time was enjoying a generous helping of fried chicken with lots of French fries and coke. I was probably jumping the gun, when I said, "The upshot of my findings on health-related issues, strongly suggest that we switch over to a completely new cooking method, whereby food either be baked, boiled, grilled or smoked. Let's do away with chillies, cooking oil, spices and gravy for good". "What do you think?" I earnestly inquired.

This news cum decision acted as a bombshell (and with hindsight I gather was tantamount to showing a red rag to a bull). Stopping in her tracks and not believing her ears, my wife zeroed in on me with gimlet eyes and pulled the trigger, "In other words, why don't you say, you are contemplating to live alone for the rest of your life!"

Dear readers, I would rather draw a veil over the scene that ensued which could be termed as pure 'Theatre of the Absurd'. To slake your curiosity, it would be sufficient to mention that my plans, alas, went kaput and I had to throw in the towel.

Television Vs A Hubby

To say that my wife is fond of watching television would be an understatement. The term 'Couch potato' better describes her, as viewing television claims a lion's share of her waking hours. She takes to TV like a duck to water and has gradually come to enjoy a monopoly over choice of channels. Channels showing movies, soaps and pop music are among her favourites and she remains umbilically attached to the (single) TV set available in our home.

Except occasionally watching sports or news channel, I generally keep away from TV room. A few days back, while woolgathering near eventide, it flashed on me that a much talked about cricket One Day International (ODI) between Pakistan and England was being telecast live. Too bad, I cursed myself for having missed greater part of the match. Bitten by the curiosity to catch up with the update on match, I scampered like a hare towards the TV room and as anticipated found my wife deeply occupied in watching an Indian drama. I asked her to navigate straight to the sports channel so as to see the latest position of the game. As soon as I read aloud the score, she made a quick scissor-like movement with her right index and middle finger and immediately reverted to the old channel, much to my displeasure.

Eyeing her disapprovingly and grinding my teeth, I spoke my mind, "Okay, you watch your choice program today, but next time, in a few days from now, when Pakistan plays against England in the upcoming ODI match, I would closely follow the game from start to finish and expect no interference and nonsense from you on that account". "Is that clear, do you read me?" I put air quotes around my words which were delivered with a fair degree of asperity. We briefly locked eyes and then looked away from each other. On the sidelines our pet cat 'Smokey' assertively signed a greeting card lying on a rug with its paw.

With an impish glint in her laughing eyes, she gave me a long searching look and in an affectedly surprised tone said, "You didn't tell me, you are buying a new TV set for yourself". Upon hearing that bizarre answer, I was dumbfounded for a while, fumed inwardly and desperately groped for words. This had her in stitches as she jocundly hit me for six, "Darling, I keep on wondering, when you would ever give up this irritating habit of being so secretive!"

Giving me a thumbs up sign and a huge grin, she promptly added, "but congrats, anyway for the new TV set, in advance". And warmly shook my hand in the manner of a consummate film actress, taking her credulous lover for a ride.

Pronunciation Issues

Most Egyptians have difficulty in pronouncing the letter 'P'. A batch-mate of mine by the name Ather was posted in the diplomatic mission of Pakistan at Cairo. After coming back from Cairo, on one occasion, he narrated an incident which took place there and went like this:

Once an Egyptian official namely Mr. Hamal came to see him at the Pakistani Embassy's premises. He came down from his office to receive him. Upon reaching the place, Mr. Hamal moved his car hither and thither, but could not find a parking space in the designated areas. While still maneuvering his car, he came close to my batch-mate and complained, "Mr. Ather, there is no place to park (read bark)".

"Mr. Hamal, you can bark (read park) right here!" Ather laughingly offered.

Conscience – Go Fly A Kite

The hearty camaraderie of a stag-party is always a refreshing occasion where you get to socialize, show your true colours and be animated – makes you feel good to be alive. *When you are with old friends, time does seem to stop for a while, and even go backwards! Only to fast forward when the magic ends. Isn't life too short not to be enjoyed as we struggle headlong in the current of our destinies?* Recently at a school's re-union party, during the course of a light-hearted banter, the conversation unexpectedly took a turn to the 'role of conscience in human life'. It elicited varying viewpoints. Boasting of leading a righteous life, one of my class fellows emphatically said, "I sleep well because I've clean hands and a clear conscience".

Hearing this, another gentleman, polishing off almost an entire bottle of beer, pulled a victory punch in the air and uttered, "I also sleep well because I've no conscience".

Dream-Man

It was dusk – an explosion of red shot with gold. I was sipping bourbon while imbibing the glory of a riotous sunset. I was, however, assailed by pangs of jealousy when I saw my wife, who is upfront about most of the things, admiringly looking at a big-sized snap of Daniel Craig (the new 007 James Bond) published in an English daily. The new Bond had become an overnight sensation and the said snap beautifully captured his muscular and manly physique, as he stood like a rock, clad in a swimming costume armed with a heart-ceasing smile.

My wife who was resting on a hammock in the lawn at that time went bonkers and putting on an air of melodrama cried, "Wow! Look at his marvellous body and sculpted good looks, I am smitten by temptation, he is my dream-man!" To cap it all was the sight of my wife heaving sighs of longing for her idol not to mention the damn snap glued to her rebellious heart. **Blimey!** Though physically present, she seemed elsewhere. *She appeared astray in a forest of beautiful illusions.* Mr. Bond had just waltzed off with my wife's heart.

Not quite liking what I heard and saw, I felt as redundant as a fifth king in a pack of cards. I punched my left palm with my right fist a couple of times as I ruminated over this insult. *Reality is but a nagging mistress that stalks us from cradle to grave… making us take refuge behind a wall of self-delusion. A man could well be married and still live under the pretence of leading a life. Is there wife after death? Is there a next level of existence?*

Cracking my knuckles and swallowing my pride as I tried to tamp down my frustration, I ruefully said, "Your sentiments have disappointed me". Then mustering up my wilting confidence, I didactically said, "I ought to be your Prince Charming, your Knight in shining armour and dream man".

Sporting a naughty smile and pressing her tongue between her pearl-white teeth, she regarded me as an onlooker regards an average work of art and then blandly opined, "My dear, compared to a dream, you personify reality and reality as you know well, tends to be bitter!"

Family Circus

Riding on the wave of a buoyant mood the other afternoon, I hid myself behind the costume of batman which I had secretly bought and suddenly appeared in the T.V lounge of my house where my family was sitting and without preamble started clumsily jumping left and right, up and down, followed by an energetic spell of not-very-impressive break-dancing. My actions could be compared to the beat of a metronome gone wild.

After noticing a lack of response (read appreciation or applause) from my family, I popped my face out of the costume and asked my wife, "Don't you agree that at times I sort of act abnormal?"

"Correction to be made my dear", she said laughing in my face, "it would be more appropriate to say that at times you sort of act normal".

French Are Great!

A mother asked her teen-age son, "Do you like French people?"

"Mom", began the teenager, "in fact, I like everything that's French. French toast, French fries, French leave, French kissing…"

Female Psychology

Having a smattering knowledge of female psychology, more often than not, I make it a point to heap praise on my wife, whenever she dresses up for special-cum-social occasions. This ego-massaging, I've discovered does women good and helps in keeping the marital climate pleasant. Moreover, it frees the male creature to concentrate on more worthwhile amusements like finer points of football game, playing chess or bridge with friends, puzzling over the intriguing laws of Physics, checking the new entries in Guinness book of world records, reading about the latest research in Genetic Engineering, comprehending the elusive grammar of peaceful co-existence, wrestling the blues, overcoming one's demons, learning the art of getting behind the masked identities and seeing the real person, figuring out how to brighten the day, finding a way to sustain a sense of meaning in life, rewriting your life – as it should have been…

The male mind, admittedly, the culprit it is, mostly remains preoccupied with mundane concerns and other practical (say unromantic) affairs and many a time becomes insensitive to subtle facets and nuances of feminine charms and beauty. The other day, before going to a party, my wife took great pain (spent two full hours in front of her dressing table) to look ravishing in her ice-blue dress and expected a cavalcade of compliments from me. Hardly aware of what was happening around me, I was happily engrossed in reading the 'Sports Page' of the newspaper eagerly updating myself on exciting sports events and personalities. "Why didn't I become a star sportsman and live in the hearts and minds of countless fans?" "Too bad!" I sadly wondered and closed my eyes and the newspaper. As my wife wasn't ready yet so to pass the time, I decided playing on the CD player the never-to-be-forgotten song "Stayin' alive" by Bee Gees featuring in the movie 'Saturday Night Fever' starring John Travolta and no sooner had the song started… I began twisting and cheering to jazz things up…

Just before leaving the house for the party, my wife – bursting with vanity griped that I had yet again failed to notice (meaning praise) her *exquisite* looks, *gorgeous* dress, *perfect* make-up, *liquid* eyes, *provocative* mascara, *bewitching* hairstyle, *superb* jewelry …**Huh!** *Gimme a break!* **I internally groaned**. Surrendering to a gentle smile, which somehow uncontrollably bursted into a mocking laugh, I merely chaffed, "You see one cannot bring oneself to tell lies every day!"

A Hopeless Bald

Some people wear their hearts on their sleeves and are warm, friendly and easy to get along. Our Urdu teacher (a completely bald fellow) during Intermediate level provided a living example of those attributes. His instructional technique and conversational style were relaxed, animated and ideally sprinkled with humour – effectively employed to enunciate a point and arrest the dwindling interest of the students. Furthermore, what really made him an instant hit with the students, inhered in the fact that he encouraged and appreciated active class participation by students, gave us tremendous behavioural latitude and believed in a two-way communication process.

One day, he was giving us a lecture and critical commentary on the poetry of a well-known Urdu poet. Prima facie, the poetry appeared to have a trace of romantic appeal and students sensing a fairly informal environment took liberty and as feedback reflective of their understanding, started ascribing far-fetched (romantic and saccharine) connotations – bordering on ludicrousness to the poetry under discussion. They embarked in a rather funny way to reduce the meaning and interpretation of the poetry to a purely puppy sort of love between a boy and girl, their escapades and subsequent tribulations and trials and in that way made a mockery of the whole issue.

Realizing that the situation was being blown totally out of its proportions and the (bad) joke was being carried too far, the educator chided, " My boys, the motif of the poetry being reviewed, in fact, between the lines, targets divine love and is not even remotely linked to run-of-the-mill romance, characteristic of our conservative society that you have in mind, where a boy driven by his immaturity and infatuation, chases a girl and in the humiliating process, gets incessantly hit by angry shoes, sandals and sticks on the head".

No sooner had the instructor finished his sermon than a voice (quick as lightning) was heard saying, "And then naturally one ends up becoming a hopeless bald".

The ensuing roar of laughter also included the (not-so-animated) laugh of the teacher.

Fleeting Glimpses

On the occasion of my wedding anniversary, I wanted to give a surprise gift to my wife and randomly went to a posh garment outlet selling ladies' clothing. Not exactly knowing what to look for I moved hither and thither eyeing various brands and styles – lost in a zoo of designs. I felt like throwing up my hands.

One of the salesgirls whose eyes had a side-long searching coquetry was keenly observing me and walking with a fluid grace came close to me, apparently to help me in making the right choice. She shot a 'Let's-get-acquainted' look and a racy smile… greeting me a shade too effusively. Stealing a glance at her I noticed that she was dressed with stylish flamboyance and radiated a sensual magnetism – a joie de vivre and had luxurious black hair that cascaded down her neck. She had chiselled features presiding over a stunning figure and her twinkling, larger than life aura carried the seductive pull of a first-rate model – looking at life with lively eyes – virtually flooring me with her head-to-toe dazzle. *Was the occasion ripe for sowing some semi-wild oats? In my mind's eye I could see both of us lounging on a yacht somewhere in the Mediterranean without a care in the world... whispering sweet-nothings in each other's ears and clinking glasses of champagne. Cheers! A self-indulgent and sensual life seemed within reach.* She was puckering her lips as if hankering for a kiss. *She had strawberry lips which if kissed could give one (**read me**) ripples of ecstasy.* **Yummy!** I smelt adventure. *Her charm seemed to work like a hired assassin – targeting intended victims with impunity. Was I facing a labyrinth... I wanted to enter, but not leave?* She further switched on her charm and silkily inquired, "May I help you? Do you have any specific garment style in mind?"

I kept quiet, blankly looking here and there without giving a reply and then my wandering gaze zeroed in on her again and an ebullient smile exploded across my face. *I stood silent, not uttering a word... just transfixed... drinking in the beauty of the girl standing before me. Wasn't I a modern-day Julius Caesar – who came, saw and was conquered? For a daft moment thought of giving her a gift-box sealed with a red ribbon (containing my heart!).*

Flashing a bewitching smile, she boldly looked into my tell-tale eyes and in a flirtatious tone quizzed, "Hey, are you here to buy anything for your wife or else I show you something special?"

Issue of A Closet

Siblings usually don't get along well especially during childhood phase and are often found engaged in squabbles and my family is no exception in this matter. Having reached the end of his tether one day, my son named Mahad bitterly complained about his younger sister called Saliha and in a weary tone inquired, "Mom from where did we get her?"

"From the closet", was her curt reply.

"If that's so, then immediately put her back in the closet", my son snapped.

Whose Fool?

Instructor: What do you call an employed jester?

A student: Everybody's fool if he is in the government sector.

Another student: Someone's fool if he is in the private sector.

Petrol Crisis…

Stuck in the middle of a very long queue of vehicles waiting to get a few litres of (made extremely precious) petrol during the recently witnessed acute fuel crisis, I was in the company of an old friend and his spouse as we languished in my car – cultivating boredom – learning to become inured to inconveniences and predicaments. Is suffering a punishment? *Buffeted by blows of an unpitying fate – life appeared to be an incoherent-disorienting dream from which I longed to wake up.* **Is life a life sentence and death a parole??!!** It is generally believed that our peace of mind lies hidden somewhere beneath the illusions of this world. Time stood still as the cars inched forward at a torturously slow pace. *People too, like vehicles, gave the impression of having run out of steam.* The sky seemed dull… life looked dismal – as if buried under an avalanche of sadness, misfortune and fatigue. *The bitter lapse into everyday life in a country (fast) becoming devoid of hope, sanity, excitement and what have you and racked with an undeserved stress and guilt. Kudos to those who bore troubles with almost classic calm!*

All I needed was a double shot of vodka and a few kind words.

To while away the time which hung heavily on our hands we listened to music, hummed snatches of old songs, surveyed the surroundings for anything interesting… *trying to spot a silver lining in a mass of **dark clouds**…* followed by a nostalgic trip down the memory lane… My friend's ability to utter something absurd every now and then provided the much-needed comic relief. All this time, my friend's wife appeared distant-aloof and remained preoccupied with reading a magazine… seemingly oblivious to our presence and the situation. She had sort of tuned out the world. *How often her hubby was able to penetrate her self-absorbed world, an inner voice asked.* With half-closed introspective eyes, I vented out my growing frustration and grunted: "Is it petrol or a perfect life-partner – becoming exceedingly hard to find".

Hearing this statement, my friend with a resigned-to-fate look plaintively said, "Likewise, there was a severe shortage of good girls for matchmaking some 16 years back so I'd to contend with whatever was available!?"

Candid Talk

Around late afternoon, sometimes my wife and I sit on the terrace of our upper-storey residential portion and share thoughts, experiences and memories. During one of our bull sessions, we had the pleasure of observing a vivid-beautiful sunset... featuring an orange-red sun painting the sky in motley of gaily-coloured hues... blending and harmonizing with each other... This subtle interplay of nature's mellow light – gradually fading away, softly enchanting colours and fluffy clouds which were sailing or rather frisking on the horizon as if proceeding on some merry mission – presented a divine creativity often left largely unobserved and unappreciated. Sunset was melting into a queer melancholy. I was in a nostalgic mood and particularly mentioned a song sung by a Pakistani singer that was quite frequently aired by Pakistan Television (PTV) in the late 1970s. I expressed my surprise bordering on annoyance that despite my fondest wish to see that song again on TV, I'd never seen it telecast again. *Well, life's like that robs us of our little joys and thrills! I subscribe to the idea that it is wise to have some Scotch whiskey as the sun goes down.*

Heaving a sigh that filled the place, I confessed that it happened to be one of my favourite songs and that it still gently tugs at my heartstrings and I became immersed in a languorous meditation, mixed-up yearnings and disengagement... *replaying in my mind James Taylor's song 'Long ago and far away'*... Slouched next to me on a couch was our pet Siamese cat. Its eyes betrayed a contemplative mood – as if musing about the meaning of life.

"That precisely explains the reason of its non-transmission" my wife said with an understanding nod – followed by a soft amused laugh. Then taking a cue from my quizzical looks, she mordantly remarked, "If it is one of your favourite songs, then little wonder, it hasn't been telecast again!"

A New Lease on Life

A married male cousin of mine who had immigrated to Canada a few years back visited Pakistan recently and came to see me one day. He is a nice chatty charmer – revealing new sides and shades of him during talk and is someone who believes in putting on a safari hat and enjoying life. He knew how to look life in the eye. What was more; he could see it winking back. His lit-from-within looks, magnetic vitality and bonhomie coupled with the gift of putting people immediately at ease and his ability to make people laugh are among his endearing qualities. He was the most exuberant, life-loving man I have ever known. A few moments of his delectable company and voila my mood brightened… giving me a heightened sense of living. He was wearing a T-shirt carrying a message 'More smiles per hour'. As we sat under a benign sun and had some snacks and tea, he invited me and my family to pay a visit to Canada and stay with them. Then cautioning me, he remarked that, "One of the first things most Pakistanis experience during their stay in a liberal country like Canada is a sort of a cultural shock".

"That's no issue", I replied raising my arms excitedly, but then dropping them limply at my side, with half a heart I continued, "Being married for a long time now, I've become immune to all types of shocks and can easily handle them!"

Regarding me with a curious look leavened with the trace of a smile, he merely gave a sympathetic nod. He left after a while giving me a quick peck on the cheek and saying, "Let's enjoy today. Hip-hip hooray!" A little distance away in the lawn, I could hear my children's excited leaps and jigs of joy as they played and I was left wondering… *wasn't happiness much like a gem buried under too much muck of daily clutter to shine. How to liberate life – besieged with the factitious cares of the world? Conclusions in life are hard to come by! Seeing* me in a reflective mood, my children and wife rushed towards me and with an adoring-caring attitude I hugged them and we broke into whoops of joy and relief. My wife punched the air with an ecstatic shout. Yeeaahh! And then looking at all of us said "To the good times ahead and let's get more out of life and enjoy the small things". Hurrah! We uttered in chorus.

Acknowledgements

The work in question owes a lot in terms of basic idea cum punch line appearing in many stories to a host of my friends, cousins, relatives, class fellows, office colleagues, my wife and children and in many instances are also based on my own observations and experiences. Two persons, however, really stand out and need to be gratefully acknowledged. They are my wife – a lady endowed with a wonderful sense of humour and Mr. Tanveer Azmi, one of my close friends gifted with a coruscating wit and having the unmistakable knack for uncovering the lighter side of things. Many pieces included in this book draw their broad source and underlying idea from them.

Special thanks are due to Mr. Muhammad Bilal for believing in my work and extending unstinting cooperation, encouragement and support.

I would like to express my deep appreciation to Dr Rizwan Basharat for his invaluable help and advice.

I would also like to convey a word of thanks to Ms Aasia Akram for the assistance offered by her in formatting the e-book.

References

https://en.wikipedia.org/wiki/Hot_Stuff_(Donna_Summer_song)

https://en.wikipedia.org/wiki/'O_sole_mio

https://en.wikipedia.org/wiki/Love_to_Love_You_Baby_(song)

https://en.wikipedia.org/wiki/Desert_Moon_(song)

https://en.wikipedia.org/wiki/I_Feel_Love

https://en.wikipedia.org/wiki/Stayin'_Alive

https://en.wikipedia.org/wiki/Saturday_Night_Fever

https://en.wikipedia.org/wiki/Long_Ago_and_Far_Away_(James_Taylor_song)

Made in United States
Orlando, FL
15 April 2022